Say What?

Inspiring and Challenging Stories from a Reasonably Well-Adjusted Pastor

DANNI & BUD -
MAY GOD BLESS YOUR
SOCKS OFF.
GO VOLS!

ACTS 20:32

Say What?

Inspiring and Challenging Stories from a Reasonably Well-Adjusted Pastor

Craig Fry

Pleasant Word

Table of Contents

Introduction

'm not usually one to doubt the direction God wants me to take, but I hesitated before I wrote this book. I've written several books before this one, and although the reviews have been positive, I'm my own worst critic. I know I have something to say, and I feel confident I can say it, but I'm much more comfortable and relaxed sharing my thoughts verbally than I am trying to formulate them on a keyboard.

So why write another book, especially one like this? Simple. God told me to. No, He didn't come to me in a vision and say, "Hey, Craig, write another book you knucklehead." God has never spoken to me that way (of course He hasn't spoken to too many people throughout history that way either). This was more of a nudge, a feeling in my heart that maybe—just maybe I could get it right this time and come up with something worthwhile. So you're left to judge. Did God really tell me to write this book or was the "nudge" a matter of self-absorption and the tuna fish sandwich I had for lunch?

My hope is that this book will be beneficial to you in at least a pedestrian way. Perhaps my daily ramblings and peculiar insights will give you a new perspective on a Bible passage or allow you to think about a spiritual theme unconventionally.

If an idea in this book manages to challenge you...it's probably the Lord using me. If, however, you find yourself nodding off...that's probably Craig forcing out another page trying to beat the deadline for publication. Either way, you've bought this thing so you might as well give it a shot.

Think of it as a personal dialogue. Pretend we're sitting on your sofa at home and we're discussing the thought of the day. That's pretty much what I have in mind and it's pretty much what I think God told me to do.

Craig Fry

Note: Bible verses and/or references are included in each story. You may want to keep your Bible nearby in order to delve deeper into each thought.

CHAPTER ONE

A Preacher and a Janitor

When I was the pastor of a church in Little Rock, Arkansas my favorite place to pray was inside the Worship Center at our church. I would walk up and down the aisles, placing my hands on individual seats, trying to remember who usually sat there. I'd pray for that person and then move on to another. Sometimes I would lift my hands in praise as I walked remembering how my heart was stirred by the most recent worship experience. If I really got carried away I'd even sing a song that especially moved me.

One day I was in the middle of one of these times of reflection, when I felt the presence of someone else in the room. No, it wasn't an angel of the Lord. It was the church janitor. I immediately dropped my hands to my side, stopped my singing and mumbled something incoherent as I slid out the side door and toward my office.

I vividly remember stopping halfway down that hallway. The Lord was troubling me with a question:

"Why did the presence of the janitor stop my time of praise and worship?"

The weakness of my soul was obvious when I admitted to myself that I was more concerned with what the janitor thought of me than with what God thought of me. And I was the pastor of the church!

This was a sad indictment as well as a wakeup call. From that moment on I determined to worship with abandon, to worship as God prompted me, to worship without regard for anyone but Him. Have you reached the same determination? If so, then Psalm 34:1 is for you: "I will extol the Lord at **all times**; His praise will **always** be on my lips."

CHAPTER TWO

Only One Song

When I was growing up, one of my favorite TV shows was "Green Acres." If you don't know, Green Acres was about a New York lawyer, Oliver Wendell Douglas, and his wife leaving the big city to be farmers near the country town of Hooterville.

Hooterville had a marching band made up of Sam Drucker, who ran the general store, and Uncle Joe, whose niece Kate ran the Shady Rest Hotel. I think even Arnold Ziffel, a pig, was in the band. Yes, television was so good and intellectual in those days.

In one episode, Oliver Wendell Douglas was named director of the Hooterville band. But no matter what song he directed, the band still played "There's a Hot Time in the Old Town Tonight." Why? That was the only song they knew.

I know a lot of Christians who are like the Hooterville band. They know only one, sad and worn out song: CHURCH RULES. Regardless of the symptom and regardless of the sin, they think the answer is CHURCH RULES. And when the rules are enforced and a person's problems remain, they try CHURCH RULES. When it fails to alter their desire to sin, they try...you guessed it...CHURCH RULES.

Jesus taught a new song...a song of grace. I highly recommend you learn it and listen to it daily. Grace is the only song that brings hope and joy and security. It's the only song that will completely change your desires. It's also the only song that reflects the heart of God. Yeah, I can almost hear Oliver Wendell Douglas singing it now: "God saved us, not because of righteous things we had done, but because of His mercy and grace" (Titus 3:5). Strike up the band!

CHAPTER THREE

My Mom, the Troublemaker

My mother died several years ago, but she lived like no one else I've ever met. For starters, she was the most prolific witness for Jesus I've ever known. Let me give you an example…

One day I went to Sam's Club (a retail outlet) to purchase some bulk items for a youth trip. My mom and our youth intern, Billy, went with me. I made the necessary purchases and stood in line at the cashier. It was then that I noticed mom was nowhere around.

I turned to Billy and said, "Go check on mom and tell her we're ready to leave." I paid and exited the building and neither one of them were with me. Billy finally walked out and said, "You're not going to believe what I just saw. Come with me."

We re-entered the building and walked to the back. There, in front of the frozen food section, was my mother and a store clerk on their knees in the aisle. The store clerk was praying to receive Christ!

When they finished, my mom gave the guy a gospel tract and we exited. Because I'm so full of grace and godliness, I was furious! My mother had embarrassed me and I wasn't going to stand for it.

"Mom," I said, "Did it ever dawn on you that some people may not want to hear about Jesus in a public venue?" I'll never forget what happened next.

My mother looked at me like I was from Mars. With a puzzled look on her face she said, "Craig, why would anyone not want to hear about Jesus?" I was stunned and convicted at the same time. Indeed, why would anyone not want to hear about Jesus? Thanks mom. Thanks for a life well lived and a love for Jesus that could not be quenched.

CHAPTER FOUR

Hope for Neat Freaks

I have to admit it. I'm slightly obsessive. I say "slightly" because my obsessions are not clinical, nor are they destructive. They do, however, drive my friends and family to distraction.

I'm one of those neat freaks who think and believe "everything has its place and there's a place for everything." This is glaringly obvious when you look at my office desk. Incoming and outgoing papers are stacked neatly and arranged by category, phone messages are in alphabetical order and appointments are written (in ink) in what my wife calls "THE HOLY DAY-TIMER."

My personal obsessions, however, do not help me in the spiritual realm. Here's a case in point. In Isaiah 55, God reveals a bit of Himself when He says, "My thoughts are not your thoughts, neither are your ways my ways" (v. 8). In other words, the plans of God are not always neat and tidy nor can they be scheduled to fit in with my tight little schedule.

God is going to do His own thing in His own way and I need to learn (as much as it kills me) to be flexible enough to listen to His directives before I plan my own. Man, this Christian thing is tough, isn't it?

So...from now on I determine to be smarter and wiser in my planning and more sensitive to the ways and will of the Lord. As a matter of fact, that's the very first thing I'm going to write down in THE HOLY DAY-TIMER...in ink of course.

CHAPTER FIVE

The Best Medicine

When my oldest daughter, Chelsea, was very young, she came down with a severe cold that had her bed-ridden for several days. Since Chelsea is naturally a very active, precocious girl it was unusual to see her so listless.

We cared for her as best we could, followed the pediatrician's orders to the letter and prayed that God would heal her. After several days, she began to feel better but I could tell she still wasn't up to full speed. On day three of her recovery, she made a classic announcement. She stood at the top of our central staircase, in her pajamas, and declared, "I am sick of being sick and I demand to see my pastor!"

Of course, I'm her pastor. But she didn't really want a pastor, she wanted her papa. And dad gum it, her papa wanted her!

Are you or someone you love going through a time of physical, emotional or spiritual recovery? If so, you that know principles and programs and promises don't comfort nearly enough. If you're "sick of being sick", you want a friend. That's the way God wired you. So right now, in the middle of this recovery that is taking way too long, listen to the heart of God, the one person who can help in your time of need: "The Lord is good to all; he has compassion on all he has made" (Psalm 145:9).

God's goodness and His compassion are the best medicine you can take. And what you will find once you place yourself in His care is that He not only gives you an antidote for whatever problem you may be facing, He gives you himself!

CHAPTER SIX

A Life Filled with Broken Hammers

I have a confession to make. I like Saturday Night Live. I know I shouldn't, but I think the show is hilarious. It's a little irreverent at times, but I like that too. What? You heard me. Christians take life way too seriously. It's good to laugh; I mean belly-laugh and guffaw and risk looking foolish. I think it's good for the soul and it's certainly good for the mind.

You see, life is tough and life's choices are tough. But sometimes we make life tougher than it has to be. With that in mind, let me share one of my favorite quotes from Saturday Night Live's Jack Handey and his segment called "Deep Thoughts:"

If you go through a lot of hammers each month, I don't think it means you're a hard worker. It may mean you don't know how to hammer.

Thanks Mr. Handey. Thank you for reminding us that we don't want to just hammer away at life and have nothing to prove for it but a bunch of sweat. I think we'd all like to make progress every now and then and enjoy this journey called life. Psalm 16:11 puts it this way: "You made known to me the path of life; you will fill me with joy in your presence, with eternal pleasures at your right hand."

Here's to a day being filled with wisdom and joy in the Lord. Here's to a lot more eternal pleasures. Here's to you enjoying life at His right hand...and please...don't let any of those folks with broken hammers drag you down.

CHAPTER SEVEN

What's Love Got to Do with It?

When I was in college, a singer named Tina Turner had a pop song that made it to #1 on the charts. The song was titled, "What's Love Got to Do With It?" The lyrics included the following words: "What's love got to do with it? What's love but a second-hand emotion."

When you examine Tina's life, it's not hard to see why she'd sing a song like that. To her, love was nothing more than "a second-hand emotion." She grew up on the wrong side of the tracks, subject to ridicule and racism at every turn. As an adult, she endured a very public, failed marriage to singing partner Ike Turner, a relationship marred by repeated physical and verbal abuse.

I wonder how many of us have an altered view and definition of love because of our past experience. How many of us are even aware of that altered view?

Perhaps it would be helpful to see the framework of love and its definition from the Bible's vantage point instead of our potentially skewed one:

1. The Lord is a good God and His love for you will last forever (2 Chronicles 5:13).
2. Even if the mountains of the earth are turned to rubble, God's love will stand strong and His faithfulness and compassion toward you will not be shaken (Isaiah 54:10).
3. As a believer, goodness and love will follow you all the days of your life and you are destined to live in the house of the Lord forever (Psalm 23:6).

What's love got to do with it, Tina? Everything!

CHAPTER EIGHT

Don't be Afraid to Dream

Tucson, Arizona was my childhood home. Tucson was a great place for a kid, especially one like me with lots of energy and imagination. I remember riding my bike up and down the arroyos (waterways that funnel rain—yes it rains in Arizona!), spending my weekends hunting for prairie dogs (rodents) and fishing in the man-made pond at the local park.

But my favorite childhood pastime was to go to Hi Corbett Field and watch the Tucson Toros practice. The Toros were the Triple A farm team of the Chicago Cubs and I remember peering over the fence and dreaming that one day I could be a professional baseball player. Until that day, my interim dream was to be the Toros' batboy.

A kid in my class told me when try outs were going to take place. I marked the date down on a calendar near my bed and went out everyday and practiced pitching, batting, and fielding grounders. I figured one of the qualifications for batboy had to be at least nominal proficiency at the game itself.

When that fateful Saturday rolled around, I put on my favorite Cubs jersey and rode to the field...only to stand outside the stadium frozen in fear. When it came down to it, I chickened out. I still think back on that day and wonder what might have been.

Do you have a dream you've been nursing for a while? I bet you do. And you know what the Bible says about that? "Delight yourself in the Lord and He will give you the desires of your heart" (Psalm 37:4). So dream your dream and step out in delight. As one frustrated batboy wannabe would say, "Batter up!"

CHAPTER NINE

God's Fingers

Several evenings ago, I was lying on my back on the trampoline in our backyard. It was an unseasonably warm and clear night and as my children bounced around me (literally) I was able to make out several constellations. This is something I hadn't done for years and I was amazed by what I saw.

This experience reminded me of one of my favorite Bible verses: "When I consider your heavens, the work of your fingers, the moon and the stars you have set in place…" (Psalm 8:3). Can you finish the thought? I'll try: "God, when I look at the vastness and wonder of your creation, I'm overwhelmed."

One of my friends is a very intelligent scientist who told me just how vast creation is. He told me it would take 16 billion light years to get to the edge of our galaxy and it's estimated that there are over 100 billion other galaxies we haven't even counted yet.

As I thought about all that science stuff and then put it together with Psalm 8, it dawned on me that as enormous as our world is, everything, I mean everything, in the physical world was the work of God's fingers. The God you and I serve today is so powerful that with a few spoken words and the movement of a few digits on His hand, all we have ever experienced was created.

Then I put my life into that equation. I realized that if God created the world with His fingers and if I rest in His arms as a result of my relationship with His Son, then I'm in a pretty safe and powerful and wonderful place.

CHAPTER TEN

Don't Quit!

One of my favorite "preacher stories" highlights the career of the great pianist and word-renowned composer, Paderewski. Paderewski was scheduled to perform at Carnegie Hall as part of a concert series for those with an affinity for classical music.

The grand venue was filled with patrons donning tuxedos and expensive dresses. Seated toward the front was a young boy, 5 or 6 years of age. As is typical of young boys, he grew restless and decided to explore...center stage! No one noticed him until he started playing chopsticks on the huge grand piano.

The sophisticated crowd was aghast. They were enraged. "How dare he" some whispered. Others muttered, "Who are the parents of this boy?"

Paderewski, hearing the commotion, entered from the wing of the stage. He approached the boy who was now terrified because everyone was staring at him. Paderewski placed his arms around the boy and whispered: "Don't quit."

And then the great pianist played a beautiful counter-melody to chopsticks.

Sometimes I feel like that little boy. Through my arrogance, pride or foolishness I wander on stage. I think the stage is where I'll find my significance and worth, but once I get there I feel the heat of the spotlight as well as the glare of those who are quick to ridicule. It's then that I'm made painfully aware that all I know is chopsticks.

But that's when our loving God comes to me, places His arms around me and whispers: "Don't quit. Don't you dare give up." And He's proven time and time again that He can make beautiful music out of whatever I give Him.

CHAPTER ELEVEN

A Frog and a Fortuneteller

D id you hear the story about the frog who went to a fortuneteller one day? The fortuneteller gazed into her crystal ball and said to the frog: "You are going to meet a beautiful young woman. From the moment she sets eyes on you she will have an insatiable desire to know all about you. She will be compelled, no more than that, she will be obsessed with the idea of getting close to you. She'll want to know you inside and out—you will fascinate her."

The frog said: "Where will I meet her? At a singles bar or concert? "No" said the fortuneteller: "In biology class."

That frog and most people I know share a common problem—we fail to ask the basic questions of life—questions that can minimize confusion and ease a lot of pain:

1. Do you know who you are?
   As a Christian, do you know the full extent of what it means to be "chosen according to God's foreknowledge?" (1 Peter 1:2).
2. Do you know where you're headed?
   Have you prepared your mind for spiritual action? Are you exerting self-control? Have you "set your hope fully on God's grace?" (1 Peter 1:13).
3. Do you know what to expect once you get there?
   Have you ever and are you now "tasting the goodness of the Lord?" (1 Peter 2:3).

Trust me on this one. Asking yourself these three basic questions and living true to the answers God gives you will keep you from being somebody's lab experiment.

CHAPTER TWELVE

Baby, You Are Looking Good!

When I was a studying for my doctorate, an elective choice led me to a short internship at an adult psychiatric hospital. I had a number of meaningful experiences during the internship, including one that will be forever etched in my mind.

A lady at the hospital would meet me at the door every day and say things like, "Oh baby, you are looking good. You are so fine! What a piece of work you are!" After a while, I started feeling pretty good about myself and I looked forward to seeing her...until one day when I saw her paying the same compliment to a vacuum cleaner. I mistakenly thought she was on staff at the hospital, but no...she was a patient!

I was reminded that the power of any message is only as good as its source. Being complimented by a "crazy person" just doesn't carry a lot of weight.

One of the great things about the Bible is that not only is the message powerful, the source is trustworthy. Since the

Bible is God's revelation and since He is the primary author of that revelation, we can trust what it says.

So when the Bible says, "I am confident of this. He who began a good work in you will complete it" (Philippians 1:6), we can know, with certainty, that God will indeed finish His work of refining us into His image. When the Bible says, "These things were written to you so that you may know that you have eternal life" (1 John 5:13) we can rest assured that our salvation is secure in Him.

Unlike my friend at the hospital, God is not confused. He has properly assessed your condition and His word declares, "Baby, you are looking good!"

CHAPTER THIRTEEN

Test Day

The Do you remember "test day" in school? It was usually on a Friday wasn't it? The whole day was a drag...especially if you hadn't studied. What to do?

a. Be honest and ask for mercy.
b. Fall down on the floor and fake convulsions.
c. Pay someone to create a diversion.
d. Offer to pray before the test, then mention all the missionaries, all the starving children of the world, all the sick in all the hospitals around the globe, all the poor in South America, and hope the bell rang before you were finished.

When Jesus was tested (Matthew 4), the setting was a barren wilderness where He'd been for 40 days. Just days before, Jesus had traveled 30 miles through jagged landscape and intense heat at an elevation of 1200 feet below sea level, one of the lowest spots on earth. Talk about a guy "ripe for picking." He had to be physically and emotionally exhausted...which is exactly where Satan began his attack.

When Satan tests you, when does he do it? Isn't it usually when you're at your lowest, when your energy level is sapped, your emotions are raw and your spirit is weak? And when you are most vulnerable, what's his ploy? Isn't it to highlight your weakness and to attack at a point where you'd never be overcome in a time of strength?

You may be facing a test today. If so, I've discovered that the secret to victory, ironically, is to admit your weakness because, "When we are weak then we are strong" (2 Corinthians 12:10). This kind of strength comes when we tap into God's power and realize our own power isn't enough. In our weakness we let Jesus handle ol' Satan. Come to think of it, He took care of things pretty well last time.

CHAPTER FOURTEEN

God's Passion and You

Did you know God is passionate about you? He must be because He's passionate about everything. Passion is part of His nature. Every time God speaks and acts He is passionate. Passion is even present in the Creation Story. God could have been businesslike about this whole creation thing. If He was, just imagine the conversation…

"Let's make the earth Son." "OK Dad." Fling…there it is stuck out there in space. "OK, now we're going to need some living things…cows, mosquitoes, an aardvark." "I don't see why we need an aardvark." "How else are we going to start the dictionary?" Yea, it could have been like that, but it wasn't!

Instead, I bet it went like this…The Trinity started thinking about creation and they all got excited! "Hey let's make a planet!" And they said, "All right!"

Then I can hear them saying something like: "Let's make Craig Fry!" "Yea, let's make Craig… but first we'll need to make his parents and his grandparents and well… let's just start with Adam and Eve." "Great! Let's surround them with horses, trees, flowers and an ocean!" "Wow an ocean...for everybody?" "Naw, just for surfer dudes in California and North Carolina."

You see, God's passion is evident from the first moment of creation! Genesis 2:9 says God made beautiful trees for us, trees that were "pleasing to the eye and good for food." He could have made sure those trees produced spinach or rutabagas but He is an awesome, creative God, passionately involved in making life fun and beautiful. That's why I believe God will give to you "exceedingly, abundantly, beyond what you can ask or even imagine!" (Eph. 3:20).

CHAPTER FIFTEEN

We Have to Vote?

My first gig as a pastor was at a church on the west side of Little Rock, Arkansas. I say "gig" 'cause some days the job was more about how I performed than anything else. But that's a different story.

My first Sunday at the church was interesting. I didn't know any better than to preach a sermon that explained that anyone could be loved by God no matter what they'd done in the past. All they had to do was turn to Jesus and away from sin. This is the core message of my life and it's something that pops out of my mouth just about every time I open it.

As is usually the case, the dejected and beaten down folks were ecstatic with this message while the legalistic folks were suspicious. When it came time to respond, the first group I mentioned reacted, as they usually do, by wanting to go much further in faith—baptism, church membership, etc.

That's when one of the deacons pulled me aside and said, "Preacher, we have to vote on these people before they join the church." Voting on members was the tradition of our denomination, but since it was my first pastorate, I'd never thought about it. The deacon's statement still caught me off guard.

I thought (and said later), "Why are we voting?" Hasn't Jesus already voted? He's the one who spoke to their heart first and "called them out of darkness into his wonderful light" (1 Pet. 2:9) and "He saved us not because of righteous things we had done, but because of His mercy" (Titus 3:4).

It's been my experience that Jesus votes for people we wouldn't, which ought to make us examine our "voting record" not His. Just a thought...

CHAPTER SIXTEEN

Whole-Life Worship

The story of Cain and Able has bothered me for a long time. The Lord rejected Cain's offering of grain but accepted his brother's offering of meat. Why wasn't Cain's offering acceptable? I mean, Cain was a farmer so giving a grain offering instead of a meat offering appears to be a natural thing to do.

Here's what I've come to understand: It wasn't the offering God rejected it was the person making the offering. In Genesis 4:5 we're told, "on Cain and his offering [God] did not look with favor." It wasn't just the offering God rejected, but Cain himself. The book of 1 John tells us why: "[Cain] belonged to the evil one...his actions were evil." In other words, Cain had a wicked heart. If that's true, then Cain's offering was probably nothing more than an attempt to appease God and not an act of genuine worship.

Sadly, this reminds me of modern Christianity. Most people think worship is one hour on Sunday morning. They go to church on Sunday hoping to appease God. Then until the next Sunday they live with no regard for Him or his ways.

We are all prone to fall into this trap. We can offend the Lord every day with no regard for our neighbors, the hurting and needy, no time for study or prayer. And about the only time we remember God is when we want something from Him.

Listen to me. What we do in a church building is not the measure of our worship. Real worship is what we do the rest of the week. And God will only accept our worship if we demonstrate our faith and devotion each and every day. That's where Cain failed. And that's where you and I may be failing too. We can do better.

CHAPTER SEVENTEEN

M. L. K. Jr. Day

My middle daughter, Charis is adopted. She is a beautiful, biracial cutie bug. She couldn't be "mine" anymore than if we were blood-related. Of course any adoptive parent would tell you the same thing.

Now you'd think Charis (pronounced "Karis") is genetically linked to me because she's so spunky and free-spirited.

This assessment was validated the first year she was in school. At the dinner table, I asked her, "What did you learn at school today, Honey?" She put her fork down beside her plate, crossed her arms and said, "Today was Martin Luther King Jr. Day...and we learned that **you white people have been shooting us!**" I almost dropped to the floor! I said, "I don't even own a gun Charis. What are you talking about?" That seemed to satisfy her until she wagged her finger and said, "Well, I'll tell you one thing. I'm not sitting at the back of the bus anymore!" This little crusader was ready to march in a parade!

The problem was not that the information she received was inaccurate. It was factual. The problem was that Charis was too young to process it. It just did not fit her life experience as a 6 year old.

I have a sneaky suspicion that God keeps some information from us, e. g. "Why do the innocent suffer?" because we couldn't handle the answer. So maybe it's enough, as children of God, to simply trust that He has a gracious plan for us, assuming that since He's God He probably knows some stuff we don't: "My thoughts are not your thoughts" (Isa. 55:8). I don't know about you, but that arrangement is just fine with me.

CHAPTER EIGHTEEN

Spiritual
Homelessness

In John chapter 15, Jesus used an analogy of a vine and branches to give comfort to His disciples. He said, "I am the vine and you are the branches, <u>abide</u> (or remain) in me."

But just how do we abide in Him? This a profound question, and unfortunately we've made the answer much more complicated than it has to be.

Think of it this way. We all know what it means to live somewhere. We live in a house or a condo or apartment. It's no mystery when we say, "I live in my home." We assume that means we "remain" or we "abide" there at least a few hours a day. It means we keep our stuff there. We have a telephone or computer and can be contacted there. It means we center our lives there and we call that place home.

To follow the analogy, abiding in Christ is both a passive and active experience. It's passive in that the roof and walls of our home protect us during bad weather and to be safe all we do is remain in there. This is a picture of salvation (Romans 8:28-29).

At the same time, living in a home is active in the sense that every day we make a decision to return home. We clean and maintain it and pay rent or a mortgage. In other words, to enjoy the benefits of our home, we actively take care of it. This is a picture of growing in salvation (Romans 12:1-3).

Simply put, if Jesus is your Lord, you can rest in the knowledge that you are saved (passive), but you should strive everyday to live true to your new identity, caring for it and maintaining it (active).

This also means (and this is life-altering) that whenever we get anxious or carry our own burdens too long, we're acting like we've forgotten where we live. I meet Christians every day that live like homeless people, wandering around like hobos carrying sacks of fear and shame. They've forgotten they are children of the King and their home is heaven!

But not everyone has an eternal home. There are millions of "spiritually homeless" people wandering through life trying to make it on their own. They don't have anything or anyone to protect them from the elements. They have to fend for themselves, which leaves many of them bewildered and begging for fulfillment in life.

The message of God's grace and the reality of what that grace means should compel us to share with them the indescribable message of love and hope from Jesus who said to all who believe: "Remain in me, abide in me, live in me...forever."

CHAPTER NINETEEN

The Greatest Moment in Her Life

Marian Anderson, an American contralto who won world-wide acclaim as a concert soloist, was once asked to name the greatest moment in her life. Did she mention the private concert she gave at the White House? Did she mention the day she stood at the Lincoln Memorial and sang for a crowd of over 75,000 that included Supreme Court Justices and members of Congress? No, none of those would do. Marian Anderson said the greatest moment in her life was the day she came home and told her mother she didn't have to take in washing anymore.

Jesus, as the Pre-eminent Ruler of Creation, could have claimed all of earth as His personal playground but He chose a different route, one of humility and simplicity. As a baby, He slept in a feeding trough. As an adult, He served as a menial laborer in a tiny, remote village. And when He died, the only thing He left behind was a pair of clothes.

Jesus' life of simplicity is worth emulating. He felt equally at ease with kings, church leaders, and the dregs of society. He never avoided anyone, regardless of their position or status. And then He went even further.

The King of all Kings taught His disciples the mark of true greatness when He excused Himself from the dinner table, slipped into a back room and returned dressed as a lowly slave with a basin of water in one hand and a ragged towel in the other.

The Master of earth and heaven, washed the feet of those He loved. It was the greatest demonstration of selfless devotion man has ever seen. It's a demonstration you and I can reflect and reproduce as we serve others today.

CHAPTER TWENTY

57 Cents

There's a well-known story about a little girl was turned away from church because it "was too crowded". The pastor, seeing her tattered clothes, guessed the reason why. Taking her by the hand, he found a place for her. The child was so touched she went to bed that night thinking of children who had no place to worship Jesus.

Two years later, the child died in a poor tenement building. The parents called for the kind-hearted pastor to handle the final arrangements. As her little body was being moved, her crumpled purse was found. Inside the purse was 57 cents and a note scribbled in childish handwriting: "This is to help build the church bigger so children can go to worship."

When the pastor tearfully read the note, he knew what to do. Carrying this note and the little red pocketbook to the pulpit, he told her story. A newspaper published her story. It was read by a famous realtor who offered the church a piece of prime real estate...for 57 cents. Within five years that little girl's gift had increased to $250,000—a huge sum of money for that time. But her story does not end there!

If you're ever in the city of Philadelphia, take a look at Temple Baptist Church, with a seating capacity of 3,300. Then look at Temple University, where thousands of students are trained. Have a look, too, at the Good Samaritan Hospital and at a Sunday School building housing hundreds of children. In one of the rooms of this building you'll see the picture of the sweet face of the little girl whose 57 cents, so sacrificially saved, made such remarkable history. Alongside of it is a portrait of her kind pastor. Just goes to show WHAT GOD CAN DO WITH 57 cents!

CHAPTER TWENTY-ONE

A Rat in the Maze

You should see how people react when I tell them I'm a pastor. Most take a second look and say, "You don't look like a pastor," which I consider a compliment, since most pastors I know are fat or bald with an affinity for polyester suits and organ music.

Now, I have a pretty good sense of who I am as a person, but other's preconceived ideas of what a pastor is supposed to look like or act like or talk like places me in a trap.

It reminds me of an analogy from college psychology class. When I was in school, we took part in a "maze" experiment. A rat was placed in a maze with walls just high enough so it couldn't see over the top. The rat's goal was to maneuver to the end of the maze where he'd find a piece of cheese...a tough task for a critter whose IQ starts with a decimal point.

But lack of IQ wasn't the main problem; the main problem was lack of perspective. If the rat could see from above, his job would be a cinch. But he can't. So he repeatedly bumps his nose into the wall.

Have you ever felt like that rat? Have you ever felt caught in a maze of other people's expectations? Are you living with a bruised nose or heart?

If so, let me suggest an upward view, one that will give you a view of life from above your circumstances and beyond the expectations of others. How about this one: "Don't look to your own understanding, but in all your ways acknowledge God" (Prov. 3:5-6).

When you look to God for understanding, He starts by telling you who you are in Him. He tells you you are loved, redeemed and so valuable He gave up His own son in order to live with you forever! That ought to keep your nose and your soul intact.

CHAPTER TWENTY-TWO

Seesaw Spirituality

The most vivid memory I have of grade school involves recess. Recess was the most glorious part of the day. During recess, I could run as fast as I wanted, talk as loud as I wanted, chew gum if I wanted and shoot rubber bands at girls! For 30 minutes I was the King of the Jungle, Captain of the Universe and the Super Stud of the Schoolyard! No one dared challenge me...except David Duncan.

David Duncan was a jerk! This conniving little weasel knew how to "push my buttons." This usually happened when he bullied me into the most dreaded playground game at Roosevelt Elementary School: "The Seesaw Challenge of Death!"

David and I would climb on the seesaw and make the proper adjustments for weight. Then we'd glide up and down like yo-yos until one of us suddenly, unexpectedly jumped off while the other was at his highest altitude. If you were the loser of the game, the consequence was a rump that stayed numb and tingly all day.

There's a similar principle at work in life. Just when you're feeling invincible, Satan challenges you to the seesaw of sin. And we seldom resist. For a while, the ride is exciting, but before long we come crashing down and injure something. . . uh, valuable.

The solution? How about choosing a different playground partner for starters? How about one you can trust! Do you know anybody like that? If you're a Christian you do. His name is Jesus and the Bible tells us that serving Him leads to a life filled with joy and a lot fewer "injured valuables."

Take that David Duncan! Oh, all right, Lord, I hear you. Please bless David Duncan.

CHAPTER TWENTY-THREE

Christ and Circumstances

What would happen if we persuaded ourselves that God's timing and His guidance will take whatever frustrated, boxed in, unproductive situation we're in and make something eternally valuable out of it? I know of one man who did just that....

Charles Simeon was a pastor in the Church of England from 1782-1836. He was appointed to Trinity Church in Cambridge. Unfortunately, the people of the church opposed Simeon fiercely, not because he was a bad preacher, but because he believed the Bible and called for holiness and world missions.

For twelve years the people refused to let him preach at any time other than Sunday morning. And when he did preach, they locked their pews so no one could sit in them. Simeon preached to the few people who chose to sit in the aisles, only one time a week, for twelve years!

On October 21, 1836 Charles Simeon lay on his deathbed and spoke these words: "I am in the Father's hands and all is secure. When I look to Him, I see nothing but faithfulness; and when I look on my ministry at this blessed church I have sweet peace."

Charles Simeon lived and died in peace because he looked past his circumstances and took hold of the wisdom and love and power of God.

The Bible says, "Be still (loosely translated: quit running around for one cotton pickin' minute) and know that I am God." So the challenge for me is to sit still long enough to hear God's voice, to be patient and learn from Him and to allow Him to teach me things that will change me into a person He can use more fully—both in and through my circumstances.

CHAPTER TWENTY-FOUR

Madonna's Emotional Treadmill

E very person has an innate drive for significance. We want our life to count, to know that when we die someone will miss us. That's normal. The question that defines us, however, is "What is the source of our significance?"

In an interview with Rolling Stone magazine, pop star Madonna made this self-declaration: "All my life has been devoted to conquering some horrible feeling of inadequacy. I'm always struggling with that fear. I think I'm mediocre and uninteresting. I push and push, 'cause even though I've become somebody I still have to prove it."

For all her fame and notoriety, Madonna is on an emotional treadmill. She thinks the only thing that will keep her a "somebody" is to "push and push" and become more outrageous. But when she grows old and in her own words, "uninteresting," what then?

Many of us are in the same trap. We may not be cultural icons like Madonna, but we "push and push," hoping our next purchase, promotion or experience will satisfy the gnawing emptiness of our soul.

Since God knows us better than we know ourselves, He knows our needs, including the need for significance. In the book of Ephesians chapter 2, here's what God says about His followers:

1. We are "raised up with Christ."
2. We are "seated with Him in the heavenly realm."
3. We now have the joy of serving as examples "to the coming ages" of the "incomparable riches of His grace."

Personally, I'm praying for Madonna. She has a soul and an eternal destiny. I hope she realizes, before it's too late, that this is what makes her "somebody."

CHAPTER TWENTY-FIVE

My Dad Just Didn't Care

When I was a sophomore in High School, I heard some seniors talking about their parents. I thought what they said was cool. It wasn't...at all.

I came home and repeated what I heard those seniors saying: "Dad you can't follow me around 24 hours a day. I'll do what I want to when you're not around." My Dad didn't even look up from his paper.

He said, "Your right. I can't watch you 24 hrs. a day and some things I can't stop you from doing, but you're in this house about 10 hours a day and I can make that a living hell. Is that what you want?"

I wonder if those seniors had ever heard anything like that before. My dad didn't care what school kids said. He didn't care what the media said. He only cared what God said. And because he knew what God said, he took parenting seriously.

I don't want to sound harsh, but I do want to sound biblical, so let me lay this on you. My primary job as a parent is not to be my children's "pal." My job is to influence them and guide them into biblical truth. I dare not shun or release that responsibility.

I don't want my kids receiving life lessons from MTV. I don't want them taking their cue from the popular culture. I know this much. If I fail to assume a leadership role in our home, somebody or something else will!

Parenting is tough. It's a lot easier to give in, but our kids are counting on us and they're watching us to see if the values we say are important really are.

Thanks dad. Thanks for caring enough not to care about anything else...except me.

Fathers do not exasperate your children, but bring them up in the instruction of the Lord.

Ephesians 6:4

CHAPTER TWENTY-SIX

Healing from Our Wounds

The famous Catholic bishop, Fulton Sheen, was in South Africa visiting a leper colony. As he leaned down to talk to a man ravaged by the disease, the crucifix around his neck fell into an open sore on the man's leg. Sheen said, "I was repulsed by the image. The holy crucifix amidst disease! And then, all of a sudden, I was filled with compassion. I reached into that sore and took up the cross just as Christ had years before reached into my diseased soul."

I can't think of a more fitting word picture of what it means to be a Christian. When the open wounds of our sin were obvious to others, when they saw our sinfulness and the diseased condition of our soul and turned away in disgust, God reached down from heaven and planted His grace in our hearts.

And now, God wants us to go out into the world where the hurting and diseased are tending their open wounds. Once we meet them there, in the midst of their need and quiet suffering, He wants us to apply the ointment of kindness and reflect the forgiveness He extended to us.

This is the core mission of Christianity...to take the message of the cross into the world as a healing agent for broken lives. So today, as you stand in the shadow of the cross, how kind and forgiving will you be? How compassionate will you be? How much like Jesus will you be?

> Be kind and compassionate to one another, Forgiving each other, just as in Christ, God forgave you.
>
> Ephesians 4:32

CHAPTER TWENTY-SEVEN

Misapplying Good Advice

My younger brother, Matt, is a good athlete. He was a state champion wrestler in high school and played on the state championship football team too.

When Matt was 11 years old, dad signed him up for our local Little League. This was a great deal of fun for Matt…until one day when he came home dejected and told us his coach had quit. To exacerbate matters, no one else was willing to take his place. The team was going to have to disband.

That's when big brother (me) stood up and said, "I'll coach your team." It sounded like a noble thought. I just had no idea what I was doing.

I'll never forget the day I shared with Matt a strategy for "guarding the plate" (Matt was the catcher on the team). I said, "If a runner advances toward home plate, be sure to block the plate with your body and don't let him touch it." This sounded like great advice coming from big brother.

In the second inning, however, my advice met misappropriation. An opposing player hit a ball deep into the outfield. He could have walked home and scored, but he raced around the bases. As he neared home, Matt stepped in front of the plate and knocked him on his keister! Matt, obviously, misunderstood my instruction and the whole team paid for it.

Have you ever given sound advice only to see it misapplied? You meant well, but the result was disastrous because discernment wasn't exercised (Prov. 17:24).

I've found that discernment is a bi-product of listening to the Lord closely and carefully. I've also found that by making this a daily practice, I stay "in the game" and off the bench.

CHAPTER TWENTY-EIGHT

Working out vs. Working for Salvation

Continue to work out your salvation with fear and trembling, for it is God who works in you to will and act according to His good purpose.

Philippians 2:12-13

Spiritual growth is a team effort between you and God. Many Christians misunderstand this. They acknowledge that God gave them the gift of eternal life, but then they think they have to repay Him for that gift as part of a performance based solo act. Nothing could be further from the truth!

The Bible doesn't say "work for" your salvation as if you could earn salvation by being a good person. It says "work out" your salvation which means to develop what you already possess. For example, if you go to the YMCA to work out, you don't go to find a body. You go to develop the one you already have.

Now this is where it gets really cool. When you "work out" spiritually, God is your personal trainer. But unlike an earthly trainer, God doesn't just work <u>with</u> you. He works <u>in</u> you:

- He works "to will"—planting His desires within you.
- He works "to act"—personally guaranteeing that when you act on His desires you will succeed.

What is our response to Christ's work in our lives? We live with "fear and trembling" before Him. That's only appropriate since this phrase means we approach Him with awe, respect and a holy awareness of who He is.

Never forget, this amazing, eternal partnership places you in a "working relationship" with Almighty God himself. He will never leave you. He will never forsake you (Hebrews 13:5). So pass me that big, ol' spiritual barbell. Jesus and I can handle it!

CHAPTER TWENTY-NINE

Contentment

There are really only two theories about contentment. The first theory says contentment comes from what you do and what you own as a result of what you do. The second theory says contentment comes from within. It's a matter of who you are, not what you do. I like the second theory best because it leads to greater emotional health and it's a lot more biblical. Let me illustrate....

A businessman was walking along the beach one day when he saw a fisherman sitting beside his boat, playing with his young daughter. "Why aren't you fishing?" asked the businessman. "Because I've caught enough fish for today," replied the fisherman.

"Why don't you catch some more?" said the businessman. "What would I do with them?" was the response.

"Why, you could earn more money," said the businessman. "Then with the extra money, you could buy a bigger boat, go into deeper waters, and catch more fish. With that money, you could own two or three boats. Eventually you'd have a whole fleet of boats and you'd be rich like me." "Then what would I do?" asked the fisherman. "Then you could relax and enjoy life." The fisherman had a puzzled look on his face when he asked, "What do you think I'm doing now?"

Try this truth on for size; it will probably help you if you're "fishing" for contentment: "But godliness with contentment is great gain. For we brought nothing into this world, and we can take nothing out of it" (1 Timothy 6:6).

CHAPTER THIRTY

An Unlikely World-Changer

art of my formal studies led me to Moody Bible Institute's Graduate School in Chicago. Moody is known far and wide as a school that stands for the highest standards of scholarship. Until recently, however, I didn't know this part of the school's history....

In April of 1855, an 18 year old man was urged by his Sunday school teacher to trust in Jesus. He did, and then soon applied to join the church. One fact was obvious. The young man did not know the Bible—at all. Having grown up in a Unitarian church, he was almost totally ignorant of the gospel.

Years later his teacher said of him: "I don't think the church ever had an applicant for membership who was more uninformed of gospel truth. This young man certainly was unlikely to fill any space of public or extended usefulness."

The deacons put the new convert in a year-long instruction program to teach him basic Christian truths. They also wanted to work on some of his other rough spots as well.

You see, not only was he ignorant of spiritual truths, he was barely literate.

The year-long probation didn't help much. At his second interview, there was only minimal improvement…but since he was sincere and committed and likable, they accepted him as a church member.

In his early years, many people looked at that young man, convinced God could never use him. In so doing, they wrote off Dwight L. Moody. But God did not write him off, and by his grace, D. L. Moody became one of the most powerful evangelists and educators in church history, a man whose impact still lives today—in me.

CHAPTER THIRTY-ONE

Say What?

- A man in Eugene, OR spoke frantically into the phone, "My wife is pregnant and her contractions are only two minutes apart! The 911 operator asked, "Is this her first child?" The man shouted, "No! This is her husband!"
- From a real court transcript (Modesto, CA)

Q: When the robbery occurred, were you shot in the fracas (confusion)?
A: No sir. I was shot between my fracas and my belly button.

'd avoid a lot of trouble and spare myself a lot of embarrassment if I just listened more carefully to what others said to me. The Bible writer James must have had people like me in mind when he wrote, "Be quick to listen and slow to speak" (James 1:19).

Keep in mind that I make my living as a speaker. I'm paid to communicate clearly. You'd think I'd remember the

71

first rule of good communication, which is to listen carefully before responding, but I don't. Too often I open my big, fat mouth and trust my brain to spit out words of wisdom. It seldom if ever works out well that way.

Why do I do this? The same reason you do it. We convince ourselves we have something so important, so substantial, and so valuable to share that others will be awed by the wisdom that drips out of our mouths. Who are we kidding?

Doesn't the Bible teach us, "Don't let unwholesome talk come out of your mouths, but only what is helpful for building others up according to their needs, that it may benefit those who listen" (Ephesians 4:29).

Think about it. How can we speak in a "helpful" way to benefit others, how can we "build others up," and how can we share something "according to their needs" unless we first listen to them well enough to know what we're talking about? Lord, help us out of this "fracas!"

CHAPTER THIRTY-TWO

Down the Hall and Turn Left

When the church I now serve first began, we had to scramble to find a meeting place. We met in a Legion Hall, a school auditorium, a convention center and finally on our own property. Each move was a giant step of faith and part of the exciting journey to which God had called us.

You know, there is something about arranging a meeting place that draws people together in a common cause and creates energy. Such was the case when we met at the local convention center.

One Sunday, the band was tuning up for our weekend celebration when a greeter had a chance meeting that defined us. During set up, we discovered that another church was also meeting in the center. Their service, unlike ours, was part of a very serious, somber and introspective year-end event.

As the band and Praise Team practiced a very upbeat, joy-filled number, two elderly ladies stuck their heads in the door. They saw the bright colors, energetic music and laughter that are typical in our meetings. They turned to the church greeter and asked, "What church is this?" The greeter responded, "This is Celebration Church!" "And just what are you celebrating?" "We're celebrating the life of Jesus!" the greeter said. The ladies looked back at him and said, "We've come to celebrate His death." That's when the greeter, nonplussed, said "Oh. Then you want to go down the hall and turn to your left."

I am so thankful to be part of a church that is filled with joy and fun and happiness. Yes, there is a place for introspection to be sure, but I always want to make room for celebration. As it says in 1 Chronicles 16:27: "Strength and joy are in his dwelling place."

CHAPTER THIRTY-THREE

Family Time

For NY lawyer Cindy Harrison, it was like getting hit in the gut. She'd stopped by the grocery store with her 4 yr. old to pick up a few things, but since the baby sitter normally did the shopping, she was unprepared for what happened. Suddenly there was her son, shouting, screaming and skidding the length of the aisles on his knees. "This can't be my child," Cindy thought in horror. Then the cashier gave a final twist of the knife: "Oh, so you're the mother."

That's when Cindy realized the myth of spending "quality time" with the kids was a farce. Until then she had subscribed to our cultures' most treasured rule of parenting: It isn't how much time you spend with your kids, it's how you spend the time.

Thankfully, Cindy saw what many of us have. You can't pencil in time with your family like a business appointment. Families need a lot of time to grow, develop and share the deeper things in life.

With that in mind, let me share some practical suggestions for beating the clock that have worked for our family:

1. Make at least one meal a day a family priority.

    - Don't answer the phone
    - Turn off the TV
    - Make meal preparation a family event
    - Let everyone share the highlight of their day

2. Use lunches for business appointments. This may free you from evening appointments.

3. Bargain for time with your employer.

    - Instead of a pay raise, ask for 3 more days off during the year for special family moments.
    - Invite your family to visit you at the office.

4. Involve your family in your hobby or leisure time.

As for man, his days are like grass, he flourishes like a flower of the field; the wind blows over it and it is gone. But from everlasting to everlasting the Lord's love is with those who fear him, and his righteousness with their children's children.

Psalm 103:15-17

CHAPTER THIRTY-FOUR

Spiritual Unrest

Psalm 1:1 says, "Blessed (or happy) is the man who does not walk in the counsel of the wicked." The root of this word wicked means "spiritual unrest."

Spiritually restless people quietly, and sometimes loudly, scramble for peace, contentment and happiness, but they never find it. Rollo May, a gifted Christian psychologist, describes this kind of person: "We tend to run fastest when we've lost our sense of direction. The busiest chicken in the barnyard is the one with his head cut off!"

Now let me ask—how many of us have allowed spiritually restless people to tell us how to be happy? What makes us think someone on the losing team of spirituality knows how to win?

Automaker Henry Ford asked electrical genius Charlie Steinmetz to build the generators for his factory. One day the generators ground to a halt and the repairmen couldn't fix the problem. So Ford called Steinmetz, who tinkered with the machines for a few hours and then threw the switch. The generators came back to life. Ford got a bill for $10,000.

The tightfisted car maker asked why the bill was so high. Steinmetz's replied: "For tinkering with the generators—$10. For knowing where to tinker—$9,990." Ford paid the bill.

There are a lot of people ready and willing to give you advice: in-laws, outlaws, friends, the media, co-workers and even preachers. The real question you should ask is, "Do these people know what they are talking about or should I go to the Lord with this one?" I think you know the answer.

CHAPTER THIRTY-FIVE

Babe Ruth's Finest Hour

Babe Ruth hit 714 home runs during his baseball career and is considered by many to be the greatest baseball player of all time. In one of his last full major league games, the Babe was featured in an outing between the Braves and the Cincinnati Reds. But this was not Ruth's finest hour. The great player of old was no longer as agile as he had once been. He fumbled the ball and threw badly and in one inning alone his errors were responsible for most of the five runs scored by Cincinnati.

As the Babe walked off the field after the third out and headed toward the dugout, a crescendo of yelling and booing reached his ears. Just then a boy jumped over the railing onto the playing field. With tears streaming down his face, he threw his arms around the legs of his hero. Ruth didn't hesitate for one second. He picked up the boy, hugged him, and set him down on his feet, patting his head gently. The noise from the stands came to an abrupt halt. Suddenly there was no more booing. In fact, a holy hush fell over the entire park.

In those brief moments, the fans saw two heroes: Babe Ruth, who in spite of his dismal day on the baseball field still cared about a little boy; and the small boy, who regardless of another's failure and shortcomings, cared about the feelings of a fellow human being. The actions of both heroes melted the hearts of the crowd.

Make sure that nobody pays back wrong for wrong, but always try to be kind to each other...

1 Thess. 5:15

CHAPTER THIRTY-SIX

My Friend Mike

Mike was one of my best friends in college. I can't remember when we met. I just remember being together all the time. Mike was a math major and I was a political science major, so we didn't share many classes. What drew us together was a shared love of music, in particular guitar music, and more in particular James Taylor's guitar music.

We'd sit around the dorm, and later at Mike's apartment and listen to J. T. and try to pick out his songs on our guitars. Mike was much more talented than I was in this regard but he never rubbed it in.

When my wedding day came around, I asked Mike to be one of my groomsmen. It only seemed right since we were practically "joined at the hip" at the time. There's no question about it, my college years were richer as a result of our friendship.

As is often the case, life took us in different directions. I went on to study theology. Mike started teaching back home in Illinois. Mike made several attempts to stay in touch, but I convinced myself I was too busy and we were too far away from each other to really reinvest in our friendship. I am such a loser!

Over the years, I've felt terrible about this...and I should. Mike is too valuable a person to be treated like this. He deserves better and I have lost someone who enriched my life.

Today I stood in my driveway and cried. Inside my mailbox was a CD. It was a collection of guitar music performed by Mike Henson, my friend! He had not given up on me, even though he has a new music career. I think I better write a letter to a friend of mine in Illinois. "A friend loves at all times" (Prov. 17:17).

CHAPTER THIRTY-SEVEN

Losing What Doesn't Matter

Tim, a middle-aged investment banker, made an appointment to see his minister for counseling one day. He had lost a lot of money and said, "I'm afraid I've lost everything."

Robert, his minister replied, "Oh. I am so sorry to hear you've lost your faith." Tim responded, "No, I haven't lost my faith. I still believe in God." "Well then," said Robert, "I'm sorry to hear you've lost your character." "I didn't say that. I still love my wife and kids. I still try to live honestly and I still have my character." Robert moved to the edge of his chair and said, "Then I'm sorry to hear you've lost your salvation." Tim was exasperated at this point and said, "I never said anything about losing my salvation. I still believe in Jesus and I trust that He loves me no matter what."

Robert leaned back in his office chair, took a deep breath and said, "Now let me get this straight. You still have your faith, your character and your salvation. It seems to me that you have lost nothing that really matters." Tim sat stunned, and then smiled when he realized he'd just heard a truth that made every monetary loss he had suffered seem like a minor detail.

Whenever I get discouraged because of a perceived "loss," I remember that story and it reinforces the fact that in Christ, I have "His divine power and everything I need for life and godliness through my knowledge of Him" (2 Peter 1:3). And if I have Christ, and if in Him I have the key components of power and life and godliness, then I have absolutely everything I need.

CHAPTER THIRTY-EIGHT

"Splaining" Myself to the Kids

My two oldest daughters were rooting around in the basement today. They came running into the house screaming, "Hey Papa! We found your high school yearbook!" This is every adult's nightmare.

As my girls journeyed through my past, they received quite a shock. "Look at your hair!" one said. The other chimed in with, "Is that your girlfriend?" Some of their other comments were directed toward the notes my friends wrote in the margins. Oh, they had a **lot of questions**: "What did your friend mean when he said _____?" "Does momma know you used to date that girl?"

Shall I continue? No!

I was reminded of the old Lucille Ball show when Ricky Ricardo's most oftrepeated statement to Lucy was: "You got some splainin to do."

I "splained" as best I could, but boy, it took every ounce of legal strategy and mental gymnastics I could muster to keep that trip down memory lane a safe one. During this whole ordeal, my brain was shouting, "What were you thinking, man?" And that's the operative question for all of us isn't it?

What was I thinking? The answer: I obviously wasn't thinking! I was in high school. My only long range plan was to buy a Camaro with mag wheels.

Perhaps God wants you to think, I mean really think. You can start by thinking about how today's decision affects tomorrow. I just wish I'd started applying the words of Proverbs 37:37-38 a lot sooner: "Consider the blameless, observe the upright; there is a future for the man of peace...the future of the wicked will be exposed."

CHAPTER THIRTY-NINE

No Condemnation

Romans 8:1 says, "There is <u>now</u> no condemnation for those who are in Christ Jesus." The small but powerful word "now" is worth noting. Let me illustrate.

A grandfather sends a package to his granddaughter and says, "Do not open this until your birthday." Every day the little girl says, "Now? Can I open it now?" "No, you may not open it now. Only on your birthday" says her mother. But when the little girl's birthday finally arrives, her mother says (and probably with a great deal of relief) "Now you may open your present."

But don't miss this. The gift inside the package, carefully chosen by the grandfather, had already been purchased. In fact, it had already been selected and appropriated specifically for <u>that</u> <u>little</u> <u>girl</u>—she just hadn't opened it.

Here's the application: Whenever a person turns to Christ and away from sin they experience a spiritual birthday. Salvation is now theirs and at the moment of conversion, they can open that gift and appropriate it as a finished work.

This gift from Jesus was finished on the cross, and **"there is now no condemnation"** for us! We can experience, through the victory won for us on Calvary, the completed work, the finished product, the "now" of salvation!

This is the gospel and the core message of Christianity. Do you believe it? I sure hope you believe it—or else you'll spend your whole life missing the awesome, majestic, amazing grace God has already given to you!

[Cf. Romans 3:21; 8:31-33]

CHAPTER FORTY

The Glory to be Revealed

Romans 8:18 should soothe the heart of every discouraged Christian: "Our present sufferings are not worth comparing with the glory that will be revealed in us." This brings eternity into our present reality, so that if you really believe God is for you and His blessings are eternal, you can draw from an inexhaustible well of strength to keep doing what God has called you to do whether or not circumstances dictate praise.

This was more than true for Henry Morrison. After serving as a missionary for 40 years in Africa, Henry became sick and had to return to America. As his ship docked in New York Harbor there was a huge crowd gathered to welcome home another passenger. Morrison watched as President Teddy Roosevelt received a grand welcome home party after an African Safari.

Resentment seized Henry. He turned to God in anger, "I've come back home after all this time serving you and there is no one, not even one person here to welcome me home." Then it was almost as if God returned the gesture and spoke to Henry in a still small voice: "I love you Henry. But you seem to have forgotten you're not home yet."

The foundation of our faith is that God raised Jesus from the dead, He reigns as King over all of earth and heaven and death and hell, and He cannot and will not fail in His purpose to "reveal His glory in us."

As a result of this certainty, we can and should bring praise and honor and glory and thanks to Him right now and forever! And if we are called to suffer for Him (even in solitude) this should not diminish our resolve one bit. Amen!

CHAPTER FORTY-ONE

Pleasing God

Any true believer in God will, at some point in his spiritual journey, ask the question, "How can I be pleasing to Him?" The answer to that question is clearly spelled out in the Bible, but sadly most people haven't taken the time to read and understand it. And if we don't understand what it takes to please God, we'll let our imagination fill in the blanks.

Over the years, people have filled in the blanks and tried to please God through elaborate schemes such as offering animal sacrifices, taking pilgrimages, or subjecting themselves to self-induced suffering. Others take the positive route and try to please God by feeding the poor, helping the elderly, or saving the rain forests. Still others try to please God through outward, religious forms like wearing their hair a certain way (long or short), or dressing a certain way, or refusing to attend or participate in certain types of amusements.

All these attempts are sincerely motivated, but they are ill-conceived. Each one is essentially flawed because they start with man, not God. In other words, they are all man-made remedies and they don't originnate with God.

The Bible tells us this simple truth: As believers in Christ we are already accepted by God because we are His children (1 John 3:1). We are pleasing to Him, because of who we are, not because of what we do.

Listen to me. Security, confidence, joy and hope are ours when we understand that we are accepted and pleasing to God by virtue of His choice to adopt us and our choice to receive His invitation... period!

CHAPTER FORTY-TWO

Life Theories

Ben Patterson, in his book *Grand Essentials* shares this theory on life. He says, "When we're whittled down to our essence, when joints have failed, skin has wrinkled, and capillaries have clogged, what is left of us is what we were all along."

Ben goes on to paint a contrast between two real-life characters in his own life:

Exhibit A was a distant uncle who did nothing his entire life but find ways to horde his wealth. He spent his life drooling and babbling constantly about the money he wanted to make and spend. When life whittled him down, all that was left was raw greed, because that's what he had cultivated in a thousand ways during his lifetime.

Exhibit B was Ben's grandmother. What did her life stand for? The best example was witnessed whenever she was asked to pray before dinner. She would reach out and hold the hands of those near her. Then a broad, beautiful smile would spread across her face and her eyes would fill with tears as she looked up to heaven. Her chin would quiver as she poured out her love to Jesus and lavished praise upon Him for all His blessings.

That was her life in a nutshell. She worshiped Jesus and she loved people. When life whittled her down, all that was left was a remnant of eternity.

I will sing to the Lord all my life; I will sing praise to my God as long as I live.

Psalm 104:33

CHAPTER FORTY-THREE

Show Her You Love Her

After years of marriage filled with constant arguments and bickering, a young man and his wife decided the only way to save their marriage was to try counseling. They had been at each other's throats for a long time and felt that this was their last hope.

When they arrived at the counselor's office, the counselor jumped right in and opened the floor for discussion. "What seems to be the problem?"

Immediately, the husband dropped his gaze to the floor without anything to say. In contrast, the wife began talking 90 miles an hour, fully describing all the wrongs within their marriage.

After 15 minutes of listening to the wife, the counselor got up from his seat, went over to the woman, picked her up by her shoulders, kissed her passionately on the lips and sat her back down. The wife sat speechless.

The marriage counselor looked at the husband, who was staring in disbelief. The counselor said to the husband, "Your wife NEEDS that kind of treatment at least twice a week!" The husband scratched his head and said, "I can have her here on Tuesdays and Thursdays."

Some people just don't get it. It's not enough to know that love is critical to a relationship. You have to show it! Trust me on this one. An outward display of loving feelings is always welcome in a healthy relationship: "Let him kiss me with the kisses of his mouth—for your love is more delightful than wine" (A song of love between husband and wife, found in Song of Solomon 1:2).

CHAPTER FORTY-FOUR

My Wife's Red Dress

My wife is such a good sport. I guess she has to be since I lovingly and regularly pick on her and use her and our family in sermon illustrations. For example, take the time she came home with a brand new red dress. She modeled it for me and she looked wonderful. It fit perfectly and accented her figure in very flattering ways.

Then I asked a question no husband should ever ask: "How much did it cost, Honey?" She told me the price and I almost passed out. "Babe, you know our church is in a building program. We plan on giving a donation to the church. How can we afford to do that and buy expensive dresses at the same time?"

At this point, I went theological (seldom a good idea). I said, "Didn't you hear my sermon last week? I told the congregation, 'Whenever the devil tempts you, just say, 'Get behind me Satan.'" Christi paused and said, "I did that...and he said it looked good from back there too!"

The story I just shared didn't really happen. My wife didn't buy an expensive dress and we didn't really have that conversation, but the joke sure is funny.

On the not so funny side is the reality behind the statement attributed to Satan. The devil always compliments us—when it fits his purposes. Then we learn (too late) that the real goal of his enticement is to ruin something or someone valuable.

Discerning Christians have learned not to listen to Satan, knowing he often uses flattery to disguise his destructive schemes (John 8:44). So whenever Satan tells you how good you look, remember the cost of his flattery is way too high.

CHAPTER FORTY-FIVE

God's Goodness

One of my seminary professors used to say, "God never urges Himself to be good." What he meant was God's nature is perfect so He doesn't need to be reminded to be good. No one needs to say, "God, mind your manners, do what's right, and for heaven's sake keep the 10 Commandments." Since God **is** good He doesn't need to be told to **be** good.

This one fact alone is a reminder of the huge gap between us and God. God never urges himself to be good, but He never stops urging us to be good.

We don't naturally and consistently do good things. We don't spontaneously share with others. Our natural drive is not to please God, but self. We must be reminded of this, and even when we are, the idea is seen as a huge sacrifice on our part.

> Don't forget to do good and to share with others for with such sacrifices God is pleased.
>
> Hebrews 13:16

The sacrifices of God are a broken spirit. A broken heart,
O God, you will not despise.

Psalm 51:17

These verses teach us that personal brokenness leads
to doing good and doing good is pleasing to God. But let's
be honest. Brokenness is not an attractive proposition. In
fact, why would we even consider it? The answer is we
won't—unless we want to be like God more than anything
else in life.

The choice to emulate God is the choice to leave self-
ishness behind, which, when you think about it, is like
saying "God, I hear You urging me to be good. I am willing
to obey You, even if it involves being broken. I'm willing
to strive to be like You with all my heart, no matter what
it may cost."

CHAPTER FORTY-SIX

Face Lifts

A "rich young ruler" came to Jesus (Mark 10). He was a yuppie and a very successful one at that. This yuppie asked Jesus, "What must I do to have eternal life?" Another way of wording this is, "Who are you Jesus and what are the rules for relating to you personally?"

Jesus gave a very mysterious reply. He said, "Sell everything you have and give it to the poor." I think this is an interesting response because it's the only time Jesus said that sort of thing about money to anybody and He said it to a guy who wasn't asking anything about finances.

Why would Jesus respond this way? Answer: Jesus knew the idol in his life was his bank account. He went straight to the heart and said, "You are worshipping another god. If you really want to follow me, leave that false god behind." The man thought about it but decided it wasn't worth it. The Bible says "**his face fell**" when he walked away (v. 22).

The phrase, "his face fell," doesn't mean his forehead fell off his skull. It means he hung his head in either embarrassment or disappointment.

Contrast Mark 10 with Psalm 3:3: "You, O Lord, are a shield for me; my glory and the **lifter of my head**." When standing before the One, True God, all false gods fade away and we are left embarrassed for having followed them. But God, because He is so rich in mercy, kneels before us, cradles our chin in His mighty hands and lifts our face in order to wipe away our tears.

If the "rich young ruler" knew that about God, I doubt he ever would have walked away. And I doubt you will ever walk away from God if you remember it.

CHAPTER FORTY-SEVEN

Christian Groupies

Christians are groupies. It's almost like a central committee of Christian leaders decides who is going to be that year's Spiritual Superstar; Christian bookstores and radio stations fall in line to promote that person's work. Christians then dutifully worship at the altar of the product selected. It drives me nuts!

Take, for example, the phenomenon of Rick Warren's "Purpose Driven Life." Personally, I like Rick and I like what he has to say. That's not what rankles me. What gets me upset is how people in the church talk about this product as if it were holy writ! We've got Purpose Driven books, tapes, CD's, video series, devotional thoughts, calendars, clothing, etc. What's next, Purpose Driven potty training?

Oh, and heaven help you if you raise the issue. You'd think you just spoke ill of the Lord Himself. This screams of gullibility and a mob mentality. Think about it. Purpose Driven won't be the last and it certianly wasn't the first marketing campaign to draw the allegiance of Christians. Remember the Prayer of Jabez? This obscure prayer was repeated by Christians like a mystical mantra that guaranteed wealth, health and blessing. Some churches even recited it before worship to invoke a visitation from God!

Please don't misunderstand. There's nothing wrong with Christian products. It's how we react to them that breeds trouble. What happened to simple trust in Jesus? Where is allegiance to the Bible the standard for belief? How about the Bible-driven Life?

Listen. Our faith is not in Beth Moore and our prayers are not offered to Benny Hinn. Exodus 20:3 reminds us, "You shall have no other gods (could we add the word 'celebrities'?) before me."

CHAPTER FORTY-EIGHT

Women Have More Brain Cells

After years of careful research, I'm convinced women have more brain cells than men. Let me give you an example. If someone pays money to sit in a football stadium on a freezing January day wearing nothing on half their body except paint, that person is a man.

Women know better. For example, I sincerely believe that if women were in charge of world government, there would be no military conflicts. And if by some chance there were military conflicts, women would feel just awful about it. They would quickly call for a world-wide exchange of thoughtful notes with flowers on the front, followed by a Peace Luncheon. Everyone would apologize and then they'd sit at neatly arranged tables and eat muffins and salads (with dressing on the side).

Because of our innate differences, intimacy needs seldom run parallel. And since we're pulled toward self and not God, the tendency, for a non-Christian relationship, is to pull away from instead of closer to our mate.

Fortunately, Jesus can unite us. He changes our hearts so we're directed toward a shared goal—to be more like Him. And when we are focused on Him, intimacy with each other is more likely (Eph. 5:31).

Since God's plan includes "life lived to the fullest" (John 10:10), happy and fulfilling relationships are not a pipe dream nor are they an impossibility. Authentic, happy and holy relationships are a reality God wants you to experience.

These questions remain: "Will you turn your life and relationships over to Him?" Will you let the Creator of Love show you what real love is all about?

CHAPTER FORTY-NINE

Billy Graham is in Trouble?

Billy Graham was interviewed on the television series *Prime Time Live* several years ago. During the segment, all who watched were treated to a replay and impressive overview of the great evangelist's many years in ministry. The conclusion of the piece was especially poignant.

Dr. Graham was sitting quietly in a chair at the end of the interview when he was asked, "What do you want people to say about you when you're gone?" He looked pensive at first, but then a smile spread across his face as he said, "I don't want people to say anything about me. I want them to talk about my Savior. The only thing I want to hear is Jesus saying, "Well done, my good and faithful servant. But **I'm not sure I'm going to hear that**" (Prime Time Live 12/17/92).

I thought about that statement for a long time. Then I turned to my wife and said, "If Billy Graham isn't sure that he's a 'good and faithful servant' then the rest of us are <u>big</u> trouble."

In reality, Dr. Graham's genuine humility was showing through and that's just one reason God has used him so powerfully. Billy Graham's heart may not allow him to flaunt the certainty of his eternal reward, but I am under no such strictures. I have no doubt Billy Graham will be welcomed into heaven with open arms and a huge, eternal reward: "Whoever wants to be great among you must be your servant" (Matthew 20:26).

Billy Graham is obviously one of my heroes and his life is one I try to emulate. Although I'm not even close to reaching this lofty goal, I strive toward it anyway. How about you?

CHAPTER FIFTY

Life Examination

Socrates once said, "The unexamined life is not worth living." When you stop and think about it, most of life is filled with examinations.

All this talk reminds me of the story of a Bible College student who faced a serious theological exam unprepared. He wrote the following note on the bottom of his paper:

Dear Professor: While I was not prepared for this exam I want you to know that I love Jesus with all my heart. I also want you to know that your lectures have been a great blessing to my life.

The Professor replied: I am so happy to know that you have committed your life to Jesus. I am also delighted to know that my lectures have been such an inspiration in your life. Furthermore, I want you to know that in the kingdom of God you will be judged on the basis of grace for which you get an A. However, in my class you will judged according to your works for which you get an F.

We may not like it, but testing is a regular part of life. Academic, medical, professional and personal tests are just part of regular living. But there is one test we should all be prepared for—the test we'll take when we stand before God and give account of our lives.

On that day, we will not be judged for our good intentions. Nope. We will be judged on one and only one criterion. Have we appropriated the grace of God? Have we embraced Jesus Christ as our personal Savior? Have we joined with Thomas in saying, "My Lord and my God" (John 20:28)? Trust me. That exam, on that day, will not be multiple choice.

CHAPTER FIFTY-ONE

Driver's License Photos

Recently I had the "thrill" of getting my driver's license renewed. Since I have a fairly clean driving record, I wasn't required to endure the questions from the little exam book or a driving test, but I did have to have my picture taken again. Oh what joy!

As I stepped up to the counter, an overweight State Trooper told me, "Take off your hat." I began to protest: "Is that absolutely necessary?" The reply was curt and to the point: "Yes sir. Now please take off your hat."

Normally, I would not have even raised the question. My parents taught me to respect those in authority, especially authority figures who are "packing heat" (carrying a loaded weapon). But on this particular day I had extenuating circumstances. You see, that morning I was running late. As I climbed out of the shower, I quickly toweled off and instead of styling my hair I just put my hat on my head. By the time I got to the Testing Station I had an award-winning case of "hat head." I still laugh whenever I look at that picture. It is hilarious!

Most of us would never select a driver's license photo to represent our outward appearance. Instead, we'd choose a studio portrait, preferably one that had been airbrushed and touched up. But neither one of those is realistic.

Over the years I've learned this lesson: If I want to be an authentic person who influences others toward the Lord, it's critical that other people see me for who I really am, warts and all. Or in my case, a Jesus-loving goofball, complete with "hat head."

CHAPTER FIFTY-TWO

Warnings about Warfare

I'm a history buff. That's why I'm fascinated by the comments of Erwin Rommel, Commander of the German West during the Normandy Invasion. In a conversation with a member of his staff he said, "The war will be won or lost on the beaches. We have only one chance to stop the enemy, and that's while he's struggling to get ashore. Reserves will never get up to the point of attack, and it's foolish even to consider them. Believe me, the first 24 hours of the invasion will be decisive…it will be the longest day."

The statement made by Rommel has a haunting echo, **"We have only one chance to stop the enemy, and that's when he's struggling to get ashore."** The Germans recognized the struggle of the allies in the water would be distracting and play to their advantage.

In the spiritual realm, 1 Pet. 5:8 warns us of a similar battle strategy. We're told to be alert because our "adversary, the devil, prowls about like a roaring lion, seeking someone to devour." Guess who that "someone" is?

In Screwtape Letters, C. S. Lewis illustrates this point with a conversation between an older devil and his nephew: "Doubtless, like all young tempters, you are anxious to be able to report spectacular wickedness. But do remember, the only thing that matters is the extent to which you separate the man from the Enemy [God]. It does not matter how small the sins are, provided that their cumulative effect is to edge the man away from the Light and out into the Nothing. Indeed, **the safest road to Hell is the gradual one—the gentle slope**, soft underfoot, without sudden turnings, milestones or signposts."

CHAPTER FIFTY-THREE

I Don't Think I Know

My first year in seminary placed me in philosophy class with Dr. Williams. The good professor was an exacting taskmaster who stressed the importace of consistent preparation. To buttress this idea, Dr. Williams would give pop quizzes.

Halfway through the semester, Dr. Williams gave one of his hallmark quizzes with a twist. He asked randomly selected students to answer a question from memory. I struggled successfully through the ordeal, but the poor guy next to me hadn't studied. He shifted from one foot to the other, stammered and finally said, "Uh, Dr. Williams, what do you think?"

I'll never forget Dr. Williams' response: "Young man, I don't have to think. I know!" Then Mr. No Study said the funniest thing I heard in seminary: "I have the same problem. I don't think I know either!"

Many of us, because of lack of preparation, lack the confidence we need for the questions of life. So here are some "answers" that will help you cope:

Life is not a joy ride – Life will deal out some harsh realities and no one is exempt! Sickness, heartache, disappointment and tears are going to touch you.

Life is not a fantasy ride – I still enjoy thrill rides at amusements parks. But everything there is controlled and artificial so I can experience the thrill without any of the danger. This bears no resemblance to real life!

The Bible is our instruction book – Why did God inspire and preserve Scripture? It's not so we can be thrilled by "stories" of the past from a safe distance. When you read and apply the Bible, you understand it is a preparation manual for real life—whether or not you meet someone like Dr. Williams.

CHAPTER FIFTY-FOUR

No Time for Negativity

I need to make two confessions. First, I don't respond well to unjust criticism. I have enough problems dealing with the criticism I deserve. Second, I don't like negative people. I mean, I love them in the Lord. I just don't want to have lunch with them. There is too much joy in life. And I choose to look for it and embrace it instead of the dreary downside of life.

My grandfather used to define a negative person as someone who was seasick during the entire voyage of life. It's like the two pessimists who met at a party. Instead of shaking hands, they just looked at the floor and shook heads.

I know I've presented two extreme responses: (1) Avoid the negative and negative people or (2) lie down and quit. I'm not big on quitting and neither is God! For proof, see Deuteronomy 31:6.

President Teddy Roosevelt believed as I do. He wrote the following words to those dealing with criticism and negative people. Perhaps you'll find them helpful:

"It is not the critic who counts; not the man who points out how the strong man stumbles, or where the doer of deeds could have done them better. The credit belongs to the man who is actually in the arena, whose face is marred by dust and sweat and blood; who strives valiantly, who errs, and comes up short again and again, because there is no effort without error and shortcoming; but who does actually strive to do the deeds; who knows the great enthusiasms, the great devotions; who spends himself in a worthy cause, who at the best knows in the end the triumph of high achievement, and who at the worst, if he fails, at least fails while daring greatly." Amen!

CHAPTER FIFTY-FIVE

Living with Yourself

Dennis Waitley, author of *Seeds of Greatness*, points out the obvious: success in our country is seen as connected to material wealth. This is nothing new. The image of shaded estates, a Rolls or Ferrari in the driveway, Gucci accessories, private jets, trips to the Greek Islands and luxurious leisure are held up as the standard of measurement for success.

However, behavioral scientists (not to mention the Bible) tell us of a deeper level of success linked to personal fulfillment. Three denominators mark this kind of success: (1) An unwillingness to accept average achievement, (2) Confidence in one's intrinsic value regardless of performance, (3) Guarding one's reputation among peers no matter what the pursuit.

In short, people who are successful, businesses that prosper and teams that win are all examples of personal integrity. When you think about it, it just makes sense. For example, does it matter if you have money or fame if you can't live with yourself?

This idea of "living with yourself" is something the apostle Paul had come to terms with. Even though he was recognized as a leader, exemplary in behavior and skilled at the craft of communication, he wasn't at peace. Then he met the Prince of Peace and everything changed, including the things he valued most. Listen to his own words: "Whatever was to my profit I now consider loss…compared to the surpassing greatness of knowing Christ…for whose sake I have lost all things. I consider them all rubbish that I may gain Christ" (Phil. 3:7-9).

You go Paul! And thanks again for reminding me what really counts in life.

CHAPTER FIFTY-SIX

Trouble on Pancake Day

Saturday is Pancake Day at our house. On Pancake Day my wife makes pancakes (or waffles) and we sit around the table in our robes and pajamas and discuss our ideas for life. On that day, the girls are given permission to act as silly as they'd like.

Today, however, got out of hand. My two youngest daughters decided to take silly to a level of personal insult. It was innocent enough at first, but with the first salvo of "You're a creepy, poo-poo head" came a series of unexpected and increasingly damaging replies, including the now famous, 'You are a whiny bag, sissy, nerd, snot licker." Uh, excuse me?

I looked up from my pancakes and directly into the eyes of my lovely bride. She looked back at me with a "You're the spiritual leader of this home Big Boy, do something about your unruly kids" expression on her face. My memory bank led me back to human psychology classes in graduate school. And I thought those classes were a waste of time. Ha!

I told my girls, "You stop that immediately. You are to apologize to your sister and then say one nice thing about her...NOW!"

Charis said, "I'm sorry. You are a good colorer (meaning you're an artist with crayons). Cassidy said, "I'm sorry. You have pretty hair."

And then, out of the corner of my eye I saw an unmistakable genetic link. No sooner did she offer the apology, than she stuck her tongue out at her sister! What am I to do with children that mirror my own attitude toward enemies? I think we're all going to memorize 1 Peter 3:9: "Do not repay evil for evil or insult for insult, but with blessing." That will make Pancake Day and every day a lot happier.

CHAPTER FIFTY-SEVEN

Words and Deeds

The little things people say can influence us greatly. This influence can either be positive and lead us toward God or negative and lead us to turn inward in disillusionment.

Maybe you've heard about the preacher who was exhorting his congregation about their role in the world. He spoke with great passion and said, "If this church is going to make a difference in the world, she will have to learn to walk with the Lord. The reply came back from the congregation, "Let her walk preacher; let her walk!" He continued, "If this church is going to make a difference in the world, she will have to learn to run with the Lord." The reply came back, "Let her run, preacher; let her run." He continued with even more fervor, "If this church is going to make a difference in the world, she will have to learn to fly with the Lord." "Oh let her fly preacher, let her fly" was the response. Finally, in dramatic fashion he exhorted, "If this church is going to make a difference we are going to have to spend a lot more money on missions." The reply came back, "Let her get back to walking preacher, let her walk."

I hope you've learned that being faithful to the Lord involves **speaking and living words of praise and obedience.** Speaking words of praise is very important, but it doesn't count for much unless we live them. As Pastor Peter Lord once said, "You live what you believe; everything else is just religious talk."

In the gospel of Luke, Jesus asked this question: "Why do you call me 'Lord, Lord' and yet you do not do what I say?" (Luke 6:46). Good question. What's your answer?

CHAPTER FIFTY-EIGHT

Southern Girls are Flirts!

When my father moved us from Tucson, AZ to Nashville, TN I was in the 8th grade. I didn't know that much about the southern part of the United States, let alone the nuances of southern culture, but it wasn't long before I was on the fast track to learning!

Take for example, my introduction to southern hospitality. For those of you who don't know, southern hospitality has its own unique set of rules and its own distinct language. I'll illustrate…

For several weeks after our move to Nashville, I thought every waitress in the Nashville area was friendly. OK, more than friendly, I thought they were all flirting with me. Why would a pimple-faced middle school kid think something like that? Easy. Every time one of these agents of Dixie kindness spoke to me, they called me "honey," "sweetheart," "darlin'," or "baby doll." What's a transplanted Arizona kid supposed to think?

Imagine my disappointment when I learned that those words were not terms of endearment, it's just the way southern women address anyone predisposed to higher levels of testosterone. It wasn't intended as a personal slight, it's just the way things are done in the South.

Maybe that's why I love the words of the Bible. They never disappoint and they are true regardless of culture. The words of the Bible are always heart-felt and heart-penetrating.

As we'd say in Arizona, try this on for size: "I commit you to God and the word of His grace, which can build you up and give you an inheritance among all those who are sanctified" (Acts 20:32).

CHAPTER FIFTY-NINE

Christianity is a Crutch

I became a Christian when I was in college. Soon after, I was in the college cafeteria and I asked the guy seated beside me if he was interested in spiritual things. He said "yes," so I asked him what he thought about Jesus' claim to be the only way to heaven. He said, (I'll never forget) "Isn't Christianity a crutch for people who can't make it on their own?"

My answer was simple. I said, "Yes." Period. I didn't know any theological arguments at that point. I was a new Christian, remember, so I thought it was a good analogy. "Yes," I said, "Christianity is a crutch. Isn't that great?" That was not what the guy expected, but his question has followed me to this day.

Why is the thought of faith as a crutch considered valid? Most people don't think crutches are bad things but necessary things. So why is a crutch a bad thing when it describes Christianity? The answer: Crutches are used by cripples and we don't like to see ourselves as spiritual cripples. It is severely offensive to our self-sufficiency and pride.

In short, the foundation of the world's criticism of Christianity is that it weakens self-reliance and replaces it with God-reliance. This criticism doesn't really deal with what is, but with what is expected.

Didn't Jesus say, "Those who are healthy have no need of a doctor, but those who are sick; I came not to call the righteous, but the sinners" (Mark 2:17). The contrast is clear isn't it? The only people who will ever appreciate what Jesus did and what Jesus has to give are those who are willing to admit they are spiritually and morally crippled—which, if we're honest, is each and every one of us.

CHAPTER SIXTY

Control Freaks

I live in a house filled with card-carrying control freaks. That's why, when my kids were toddlers, I had to clean cereal off the wall every morning. As I approached their mouths with a spoonful of cereal, they would swing around and send the cereal flying!

They were all control freaks. They wanted to decide when it was time to eat, what they would eat, when they got their diapers changed and on and on.

The fact of the matter is I'm a control freak too. I like to be behind the wheel of the car instead of the passenger seat. I like to hold the TV remote control. I like to customize (a euphemism for control) the settings on my computer. I'm a control freak.

These examples sounds like no big deal, but being a control freak can get ugly when we try to control things that are impossible to control. How about when we trust our spiritual status to our own efforts? Committing to read the Bible more, pray more, attend church more, or give more money to church are all good, spiritual activities. But these have no eternal effect unless we relinquish control of our lives to God and rest in complete dependence on Christ.

God is responsible for our spiritual position; we are responsible for giving up control and resting in His ability to live His life in and through us: "The God who started this great work in you will keep at it and bring it to a flourishing finish on the very day Christ Jesus appears" (Phil. 1:6, Message).

Who will bring it to a flourishing finish? God said He will. God's job description is that He runs things. So how 'bout we trust Him to do His job? He's real good at it.

CHAPTER SIXTY-ONE

Worshiping our Traditions

We all have our traditions. At our church, we end every worship service by standing and "joining hands across every aisle." We are not a tradition-laden church by any stretch, but I have a sneaky feeling if we deviated from this parting gesture there would be a mutiny. It's a harmless tradition and we have no intention of imposing it on others as a test of faith. Other traditions aren't quite so harmless.

If we're not careful, "the way we do things" can become a demand that others do it our way or else. In relationship with and in response to other Christians, traditions can be especially unhealthy. Why?

Mark 7 warns that our traditions can become a test of acceptability (vv. 1-5). And when we measure others by our own personal convictions instead of the objective standard of Scripture, we fall victim to a slick satanic trap. When adhering to a tradition becomes a measure of spirituality (vv. 6-7), we've lost sight of our eternal goal, which is to please God and God alone. As I read it, the Bible says the goal of the Christian life is not to <u>look</u> right <u>for</u> God, but to <u>be</u> right <u>in</u> God.

What does Jesus call for? He expects a radical reorientation of our lives and a concern for how things really are. So if you have a heart for God, and if your heart beats for truth as His does, then and only then will you be free from the counterfeit of tradition:

> The God who made the birds doesn't make birdcages; it is men who make birdcages, and after a while we become cramped and can do nothing but chirp and stand on one leg. When we get into God's great free life, we discover that that is the way God means for us to live.
>
> Oswald Chambers

132

CHAPTER SIXTY-TWO

The Prodigal Father

Jesus never gave this story a title, but the most popular title over the years has been "The Prodigal Son." Interestingly, the definition of the word prodigal has been lost to some extent. According to Webster, the word means: "Recklessly extravagant; characterized by wasteful expenditure; Lavish and yielding abundantly; luxuriant."

When you think about the characters in this story, it becomes obvious that **the father is the prodigal, not the son.** The father was extravagant in the way he ran to his son. The father was lavish in giving a robe and a ring. His decision to kill the prized calf could be called a wasteful expenditure. The feast was an abundance of food. When this son, who had been a disrespectful jerk, returned home, the father spared no expense to display his mercy and grace.

Our labeling of the "Prodigal Son" makes it easy to miss a core truth: This is not a parable about the son as much as it is a parable about the Father. That's right. It's the Father who plays the lead role. The story begins, "A certain man had two sons…" Had it been a story about the son, it would read, "A certain young man had a father and a brother. . ."

God, our Father, is the preeminent Prodigal. He is extravagant with His love. He is lavish with His grace. He wants us to have a spiritually abundant life.

He has every right to deal harshly with us when we turn our back on Him and dishonor Him. But He does not. He welcomes us home. He runs to meet us. He showers us with His outrageous grace and mercy. And we gladly honor and follow Him now because He first loved us (1 John 4:19).

CHAPTER SIXTY-THREE

The Beatitudes Revisited

Then Jesus took his disciples up to the top of the mountain and gathered them around. He taught them saying:

BLESSED ARE THE POOR IN SPIRIT, FOR THEIRS IS THE KINGDOM OF HEAVEN.
BLESSED ARE THE MEEK.
BLESSED ARE THEY THAT MOURN.
BLESSED ARE THE MERCIFUL.
BLESSED ARE THEY WHO THIRST FOR JUSTICE.
BLESSED ARE YOU WHEN PERSECUTED.
BLESSED ARE YOU WHEN YOU SUFFER.
BE GLAD AND REJOICE, FOR YOUR REWARD IS GREAT IN HEAVEN.

Then Simon Peter said, "Do we have to write this down?" And Andrew said, "Are we supposed to know all of this?" And James said, "Will we have to take a test on this?" And Phillip said, "I'd love to record this, but I don't have any paper." And Bartholomew said, "Do we have to turn this in any time soon?"And John said, "The other disciples didn't have to learn this, why do we?"And Matthew said, "I have to potty. Can I go to the bathroom? And Judas said, "What does this have to do with real life?"

Then one of the Pharisees asked to see Jesus' lesson plan and inquired of Jesus, "What are your objectives in the cognitive domain and what are your plans for remediation of the human collective?"

JESUS WEPT.

CHAPTER SIXTY-FOUR

Conversational Prayer

I love to pray. I relish the time spent pouring out my innermost thoughts to the One who put those thoughts in my head in the first place. In prayer, I sense God's pleasure and I feel His presence in my life. If I experience all of this in prayer, why is it so difficult to convince other people to pray?

Part of the answer at least is found in the way some Christians define prayer. When some folks describe prayer, they make it so complicated, regimented and rehearsed, I'm not sure I know what they're talking about.

When you break it all down, prayer is simple. It's a conversation. Granted, it's a conversation with the Creator of the entire universe, but it's a conversation nonetheless. Recognition of this fact alone is enough to fuel passion for dialogue—God desires that we access His throne room and His heart!

He tends His flocks like a shepherd. He gathers the lambs
in His arms and carries them close to His heart.

Isaiah 40:11

God's heart is the place where we find love and
acceptance (Ephesians 3:17-18), which provides the perfect
backdrop for "approaching the throne of grace with confidence...to receive mercy and find grace to help us in our
time of need" (Hebrews 4:16).

So talk to Him! Tell God everything you would a close
and loving friend. Listen to His voice through the Bible
and respond to the thoughts and feelings His Spirit plants
in your heart.

A simple but life-changing conversation with the
Designer of the World is just a prayer away. Yes, it that's
simple and it's that powerful.

CHAPTER SIXTY-FIVE

Lord, Have Mercy!

In Jesus day, mercy was not a virtue. It was something to be scoffed. For example, a land-owner had absolute authority over his slaves. They were seen as property. A father had literal life and death authority over his children, even to the point of condemning a disabled or deformed child to death. In this setting, the Roman Emperor was admired for his ruthlessness as much as any edict he produced.

Boy things have changed. Or have they? In our day, mercy doesn't fare much better. We applaud the sports hero who jams the ball "in your face." Our movies glorify the vigilante who seeks justice by blowing the villains head off. Business deals are lauded when someone "sticks it to" the competition.

I don't think there's any question that the biblical idea of mercy puts us at odds with the world, but mercy is not an option, it is an absolute necessity for our testimony.

Mercy is more than an honorable emotion. It is more than just a valued principle. Mercy is the slender nerve that binds our hearts to God and gives evidence that we share His values.

Be mindful of the fact that mercy drew Jesus into our lives. He left heaven and came to earth because we had dirty hearts that were in desperate need of being changed. And only a merciful God would knowingly and willingly get His hands dirty in order to make our hearts clean:

> In all their distress He too was distressed, and the angel of His presence saved them. In His love and mercy He redeemed them; He lifted them up and carried them.
>
> Isaiah 63:9

CHAPTER SIXTY-SIX

Sun-Judged

Philippians 1:10 says God works in our lives in order to make us genuine people. To describe this genuineness, Paul used a very interesting word. He says Christians are made pure or "sun-judged."Let me explain why this is so interesting.

In Paul's day, dishonest sculptors would take defective or inferior statues and fill in the cracks and blemishes with wax. Paint would then be applied, further concealing the flaws.

To the casual glance there didn't appear to be a problem. And they would be sold "as is."

In time, however, the heat of the sun would melt the wax and reveal the inferior quality of the product and its workmanship (to say nothing of the scruples of the sculptor). So when Paul spoke about being "sun-judged" he was referring to something or someone who had been thoroughly tested by the heat of adversity and found to be genuine.

This level of purity and genuineness is a goal every one of us should strive to reach. It reminds us that God wants us to be the "genuine article" in all we say and do. God designed us to be who we are, not someone we'd rather be.

The good news of the gospel is that God loves you just the way you are. He also loves you too much to leave you that way. So allow His Spirit to transform your soul. Let His love shore up your insecurities, and rest assured that when God touches your life, the finished product will be **the real deal**.

CHAPTER SIXTY-SEVEN

Jesus and the Old Testament

A new convert entered a Christian bookstore to purchase a Bible. The sales clerk asked, "What kind of Bible would you like?" The woman replied, "I want one where everything Jesus said is in red ink." The clerk returned with a beautiful, leather-bound Bible. The customer took the Bible out of the box and began to thumb through the Old Testament. After a while, she said, "He didn't have too much to say, did he?"

The case can be made that Jesus had plenty to say in the Old Testament. In fact, He's the primary subject of much of the Old Testament. He is present at creation (Genesis). He is the suffering servant who paid the penalty for our sins (Isaiah). He is our comforter (Psalms). He is the messenger of a brand new covenant with God (Malachi).

This Old Testament truth was transferred to Jesus' earthly ministry. In Matthew 5, for example, Christ said, "I came to **fulfill the Old Testament**, not destroy it." Those words serve as a marker to set Jesus apart as the sole, qualified interpreter of the Old Testament. The best understanding is that Jesus "fills up" the requirements of the Old Testament by providing in Himself the full revelation of it's meaning.

You may remember that one of the purposes of the Old Testament was to point us to the promised Messiah. In fact, the meaning of the Hebrew word for Torah (Book of Law) is "to point or direct."

Jesus identifies Himself as the living and true expression of all the core promises of the Bible, the long awaited Messiah and the sole authoritative interpreter of God's plan for us. As such, He is the One worthy of our worship!

CHAPTER SIXTY-EIGHT

Borrowing Pots and Pans

There is a great story in 2 Kings 4 about a widow who needed a miracle. She was in deep financial trouble when she told the prophet Elisha, "All I have is a little bit of oil." In a step of faith, and in obedience to the man of God, she rounded up all the pots and pans she could find and placed them on her kitchen floor.

As she poured the oil from her little pot, God somehow multiplied and multiplied that oil until every vessel was filled! She sold the oil, paid off her debts and lived the rest of her life off the leftovers.

Don't miss the faith of the widow in all of this. Asking your neighbors for empty vessels, is a test of faith, especially when you don't have anything to put in them. And when she placed those vessels on the floor and prepared to obey, she must have thought, "What if God doesn't come through for me?"

1. She'd have to return all those vessels back to her neighbors and tell them that God didn't fill them

with oil and the prophet probably was a little off balance.

2. Her home would now be the target of ridicule.

But none of those fears were realized. God did come through, just as the prophet said He would. And the simple message of the story is: if God asks for empty vessels, He is going to fill them!

I want to be more like that faithful widow. I am sometimes skeptical and can't see how God is going to work things out.

Why can't I see it more often than I do? The answer is I forget how faith works. Faith is trusting God to be God—which has little (if anything) to do with my figuring it out. It's a simple proposition really. Do I trust God or not? Now that I think about, do you mind if I borrow a few pot and pans?

CHAPTER SIXTY-NINE

Mosquito-Sized Faith

God has always taken small measures of faith and made them huge!

Example #1: One day Jesus took 5 donuts and 2 tiny sardines from a little boy's lunch and used it to feed well over 5,000 people.

Example #2: One day God asked Moses, "What is that in your hand?" and Moses said, "It's a stick." But that stick became more than a stick. It was a symbol God used to bring plagues upon Egypt. It became a serpent before the eyes of Pharaoh. It opened and closed the Red Sea. And it brought water out of a rock for 6 million people!

Example #3: One day God told Samson to take the jawbone off a donkey's carcass and use it as a weapon to kill 1000 Philistines, the enemies of Israel.

Here's the application: Never think that what you have to offer God is insignificant. You may not think you are the best singer or speaker or parent or friend or resource, but the question remains: Didn't God speak to you? He could have chosen someone else, but He chose to tell you His plan.

I love to tell people, "If you think smallness equals lack of influence you've never been in bed with a mosquito!" Think about it.

Someone a lot smarter than me put it this way: "God is not only the Master of Ceremonies; He's the Master of Circumstances!"

God can take your circumstances and perform miracles in the midst of them. How much or how little you have doesn't matter one bit! The only thing that matters is that you surrender what you have to God!

CHAPTER SEVENTY

Joey's Attitude

An elder in my church wrote to me about Joey, a natural motivator. Each morning Joey says to himself: "I have two choices today. I can choose to be in a good mood or a bad mood. I choose to be in a good mood. Each time something bad happens, I can choose to be a victim or learn from it. I choose to learn from it. Every time someone complains, I can choose to accept it or I can point out the positives. I choose the positive side of life."

Several years ago Joey was involved in a serious accident, falling some 60 feet from a tower. After 18 hours of surgery and weeks of intensive care, Joey was released from the hospital. "When I was on the ground, I remembered that I had two choices: I could choose to live or I could choose to die. I chose to live. The paramedics kept telling me I was going to be fine. But I saw the expressions on the faces of the doctors and nurses. In their eyes, I read 'he's a dead man'. I knew I needed to take action. A few minutes later a nurse asked if I was allergic to anything. 'Yes, I said. ' The doctors and nurses immediately stopped working waiting for my reply. I took a deep breath and said, 'Gravity.'"

Over their laughter, I told them, "Now listen up. I am choosing to live. Operate on me as if I am alive, not dead."

Joey lived, thanks to the skill of his doctors, the prayers of the folks in his local church, and his amazing attitude.

Every day we can choose to live fully, just like Joey does. We can claim Psalm 36:9 for ourselves: "For with you [God] is the fountain of life; in your light we can see light."

CHAPTER SEVENTY-ONE

Success and Failure

The vantage point of the world and the vantage point of the cross are miles apart. As proof, consider that from the world's vantage point the success story among the apostles was Judas and the complete failure was Peter.

Judas was a success in ways that often impress us: he was successful financially and politically. He cleverly arranged to control the money of the apostles and he skillfully manipulated the political forces of the day to accomplish his goal.

Peter was a failure in ways that we most dread: he was weak in a crisis and he was socially inept. At the arrest of Jesus he was a hapless, blustering coward; in the most critical situations of his life he said the most embarrassingly inappropriate things. He was not the company we'd want with us in times of danger, and he was not the kind of person we'd feel comfortable with at a social occasion.

But time has reversed our judgments on these two men. Judas is now seen as synonymous with betrayal while Peter is one of the most honored names in the church. Judas is seen as a villain; Peter is seen as a saint.

Sadly, the unregenerate world continues to chase after the so called "success" of Judas: financial wealth and political power. At the same time, the world braces itself against the "failures" of Peter: total dependence on God and an awareness of the weaknesses of self. When will we ever learn that true success only comes when we change our vantage point to match God's?

CHAPTER SEVENTY-TWO

Beyond the Tithe

Several years ago my Dad wrote a book titled, Beyond the Tithe. In that book, he tells the story of a generous, well-to-do farmer who loved the Lord and believed it was better to give than receive. One day a neighbor came to his house and asked him how he could give so much to others and still remain prosperous. "That's simple," said the farmer. "I shovel out what God shovels in, and God has a much bigger shovel than I do!"

That farmer was modeling the principle found in Malachi 3: "Test me in this, says the Lord Almighty, and see if I will not throw open the floodgates of heaven and pour out so much blessing that you will not have room enough for it" (v. 10).

Later in that same book my Dad told the story of a city boy who was visiting his country cousins. The cousins were trying to teach him to milk a cow. As the young man returned from the barn, his uncle asked, "How much did 'Ol Bessie give us today?" The boy sighed and said, "She didn't give anything. I had to squeeze every drop of it out of her."

There aren't many things worse than trying to squeeze or coerce a Christian into giving their time and money. In fact, it's counterproductive and only leads to guilt and resentment.

The simple fact is God has blessed each of you to one degree or another. In relationship to Him as the Source of blessing, He either has possession of your heart or He doesn't. If He owns your heart you'll want to bring Him glory and one of the things that glorifies Him most is giving, loving and living sacrificially.

CHAPTER SEVENTY-THREE

Deep Theology

I've studied theology for years, and the more I study the more I'm convinced that good theology is all about proper definitions. How we define ideas directly influences the understanding and utilization of those ideas. A case in point is the often used word "deep" to describe a spiritual experience such as "that was a deep sermon" or "that kind of teaching is too deep."

But what does "deep" mean? Usually when I ask someone to define what they mean by "deep" they are at a loss for words. I query further, "Was it deep because we explored key Greek or Hebrew words? Was it deep because we spent more time on the historical background of the text? Do you mean deep in the sense that we looked at a biblical truth from a new angle you hadn't considered before?" This line of questioning is often met with silence, a shrug of the shoulders or "I dunno."

Is it safe to assume that the idea of "deep" is a good thing? I'd say the answer is "yes," but I've concluded that deep is whatever the speaker wants it to mean, which just confuses anyone listening.

Perhaps we'd be better served by defining deep as something that touches what God expects of us. "What does the Lord expect of you?" we're asked in Micah 6:8. "He has showed you what is good (could we exchange the word deep?)...to act justly, to love mercy and to walk humbly with your God."

I have a feeling that if we are living justly and in mercy and in humility before the God with whom we relate personally, a lot more of life and a lot more of our worship would have spiritual weight. Now that's deep!

CHAPTER SEVENTY-FOUR

There are No Atheists

Jim and Tonya wanted me to officiate their wedding. I didn't know either one of them very well, so I asked about their spiritual position. Tonya said she was a Christian. Jim said he was an atheist.

I turned to Jim: "You're a likable guy Jim, but you're not an atheist." He said, "I know what I am. I'm an atheist." "No you're not. It's not intellectually plausible to be an atheist." "Prove it" he said.

I responded: "You seem like a very intelligent fellow. Do you know everything there is to know about everything? Have you experienced everything in the entire universe?" "Of course not" Jim replied.

"Well," I said, "let's say you know and have experienced half of everything there is in the universe. That would be great, don't you think?" Jim said, "It would be impossible, but yes." I paused and said, "If that were true, you'd have to admit God could exist in the half you don't know."

Jim let that sink in: "Whoa. You're right. I guess it's not possible to be an atheist."

"So," I said, "are you a soft agnostic or a hard agnostic?" Jim said, "I don't know. A few minutes ago I thought I was an atheist!"

After explaining the difference, Jim decided he was probably a soft agnostic. That's when I held up my hand, my fingers a few inches apart. I said, "You are this close to becoming a Christian."

After a few months and several casual lunch discussions that's exactly what happened. Jim became a Christian. A few months after that, I officiated their ceremony and we are still very close friends. "Always be ready to make a defense for your faith" it says in 1 Peter 3:15. It also helps make a pretty good marriage.

CHAPTER SEVENTY-FIVE

Don't Miss It

Michal stood there, spectator to one of the most glorious moments in history. The Ark of the Covenant, long held by the Philistines, was back in Jerusalem. Leading the procession was her husband, King David. Caught up in the exuberance of the moment, David cast aside all concern for personal dignity as well as most of his clothes! He donned a simple prayer cloth (ephod) and joyfully danced before the Lord. You heard me—he danced!

A party broke out! The people shouted, the trumpets blared and the crowd went crazy! And what was Michal's reaction? She wanted no part of it, no sir! When David came home, disgust was written all over her face. Sarcasm dripped from her tongue as she said, "My, how the King of Israel distinguished himself today" (2 Samuel 6:20).

Do you see the contrast? David's actions were motivated by praise for God and **personal humility**. All Michal saw was the absence of decorum. David was motivated by a consuming praise for God without any thought of how it would affect his reputation: "I will celebrate before the Lord. I will become even more undignified than this, and humiliated in my own eyes" (vv. 21-22).

The Ark of the Covenant (the place of God's glory) had come back home to Jerusalem, but Michal refused to celebrate. "Why, what would the slave girls say?" (v. 20) was her only response.

What a tragedy. God came to town, the Lord was at hand and Michal was unmoved by Him! It was a marvelous, glorious, magnificent day to praise God, but Michal missed it. Just make sure you don't.

CHAPTER SEVENTY-SIX

Pirates of Praise

There they stood, looking like they'd just come from a lemon-sucking contest. They had obvious disdain for this strange, circus-like parade winding its way through the city. The crowd shouted, "Hosanna!Hosanna!" as they spread palm branches and clothing in the road. And for whom was this parade given? Was it a governor or a king? No. All of this was in honor of an unemployed carpenter—on a donkey!

Of course, this wasn't just any carpenter, this one, the one called Messiah, threatened their carefully constructed system of rituals and traditions. So they cried out, until finally their voices were heard over the pandemonium. They demanded that Jesus rebuke His followers for their unseemly display. But Jesus was having none of that!Since He saw things from an eternal perspective, He said, "No way. I wouldn't think about silencing their praise. You see, if they don't shout for me, the rocks will!" (Luke 19:40).

Don't misunderstand. The Pharisees were not bad people. Most "pirates of praise" aren't. They see themselves as protectors of the sacred. But in the end, the Pharisees idea of worship had a lot more to do with technical correctness than intimate, personal devotion to God.

The Pharisees, like many Christians today, were so consumed with religious duty and church tradition they failed to see that the object of their spiritual devotion stood right in front of them. They were eye-to-eye with the One they'd longed for and prayed for and they didn't even recognize Him.

CHAPTER SEVENTY-SEVEN

Party Pooper

He stood in the field, leaning on a shovel, with an expression on his face that would sour milk. The farm had been transformed into a carnival, a carnival he had no intention of attending. His father pleaded with him, but he wanted no part of it. After giving his "poor pitiful me" speech, the father answered his bitter reply with these words: "**We had to celebrate**" (Luke 15:32).

The older brother wanted nothing to do with this celebration. Do you know why? I bet you do. The return of his younger brother was a celebration of grace, a concept the older brother didn't want to understand. Like a lot of well-intentioned Christians, he thought people should get what they deserve, nothing more, nothing less and nothing else.

The speech he gave his father (vv. 29-30) revealed his heart. He thought he'd gotten "the short end of the stick." And he was right you know. Little brother didn't deserve the reception, the new robe, the ring, or the feast. But the real tragedy is that the older brother didn't realize that this was a demonstration of his father's love. He had lost nothing. In fact, he could access the same love anytime he wanted!

It's been my experience that the greatest expressions of praise often come from those who have the deepest hurts, those who've drawn deepest from the well of God's grace; those who are broken and bruised and need healing. And isn't that usually when the Healer shows up?

Oh, it was a great day to revel in God's mercy, but the older brother missed it. I wonder how many expressions of God's grace you've missed lately.

CHAPTER SEVENTY-EIGHT

Your Playing Partner

Anyone who knows me knows that I love to play golf. I'm a golf nut. In fact, while I'm typing this, I'm also watching the first round of the Master's golf tournament on television.

Golf will teach you a lot of life lessons and one of the first things you learn about golf is that it is a game you can never conquer. For example, those of you who don't know much about golf (and I seriously question your salvation if you don't), hitting the ball where you want it to go is one of the hardest things you could ever try to do. In golf language, if you hit the ball to the right it's called a "slice." If it goes to the left it's called a "hook." And if it goes straight, it's called a miracle. What does this have to do with the Christian life? Hang on…its coming.

The first time I ever played golf was in Franklin, TN. Our church sponsored a "4-Man Scramble." Four guys form a team and you get to play the best ball anyone in your group hits. I was paired with three good golfers, including a guy who was the Teaching Pro at the local country club. Man was he good!

Being paired with this guy meant I didn't have to worry—at all. If my ball wound up in the lake so what? I could walk up to where Mr. Pro Golfer's ball landed and hit from there. It was wonderful!

It dawned on me about halfway through the round that this is a parallel with the Christian life and how it's lived. You see, every Christian has a "playing partner" named Jesus. The Bible says we are flawed and sinful (for purposes of the analogy—we hit hooks and slices all day long) but the Bible also says if we have a personal relationship with Jesus, He lives in us and walks beside us and goes before us, so that the game of life is decided not only by how well we play, but more importantly by how well He has played.

Do you see it? I sure hope you do, because until you come face-to-face with the sufficiency of Christ and the deficiency of self, you will struggle with shame, hopelessness, and despair. If you are a Christian, Jesus Christ is your playing partner. And it is through His sacrifice and His decision to rescue you from sin that you are saved:

> Salvation is found in no one else, for there is no other name under heaven given to men by which we must be saved.
>
> Acts 4:12

CHAPTER SEVENTY-NINE

Cootie Shots and the Hormone Fairy

Do you remember the first time you noticed the opposite sex? I do. I can also remember that my first thought was that girls weren't all that special. In fact, I used to get "cootie shots" to protect me from all those "scum queens." Did you?

But then strange things started happening to me in the 7th grade. That's when the "Hormone Fairy" came to visit and she left me some pretty significant gifts just to remind me she'd been there. First, my voice started to sound like a roller coaster. Second, I got a cheesy little pencil-thin mustache (kind of like the one grandma had). Third, my hormones started bouncing around like ping-pong balls in a microwave.

Anyway, after the Hormone Fairy came to visit, girls started looking different and I started feeling different. Suddenly, I didn't mind "cooties" anymore. In fact, I looked forward to them. What was I supposed to do with these urges?

You might think this is a discussion for teenagers but it's not. All of us (even adults) better learn to deal with the opposite sex in healthy, biblical ways.

Oh, I could give you statistics about sexually transmitted diseases and pregnancy and try to scare you into purity. And it would work—for a while. But the only way to really maintain sexual purity is to: (1) respect yourself and (2) fall in love with Jesus. Trust me. It works!

When you fall in love with Jesus and when you understand the beautiful, God-ordained design of your sexuality, then anything the world offers will be seen as a cheap substitute for the real thing (Psalm 85:8-10). Yeah, the Hormone Fairy can mess with your body, but God can transform your heart!

CHAPTER EIGHTY

Living the Promises

Tom Long relates a story that changed his way of thinking about church and faith. He was a student at Princeton University when he visited a nearby Presbyterian church that prided itself on being a liturgical, academic and intellectual church.

Early on, Tom attended a church family supper and sat down next to an older gentleman, introduced himself, told him he was new, and said, "Have you been a member of this church long?"

"Oh yes," the man said. "In fact I was here long before this became such a scholarly church. Why I'm probably the only non-intellectual left in the membership. I haven't understood a sermon in over 25 years."

"Then why do you keep coming," Tom asked?

The man replied, "I come to this church because every Monday night a small group of us gets in the church van and drives over to the local Youth Correctional Center. Sometimes we play basketball, ping-pong or some other game. Usually we share a Bible story and pray with them.

But mostly we just get to know these kids and listen to their problems.

"I started going to the Center because Christians are supposed to do those kinds of things and this church gives me the opportunity. But now I could never stop. Sharing the love of God at that Youth Center has changed my life forever."

Then he shared this profound statement: "It's very difficult to prove, intellectually, all the promises of God, but if you live them, others will see that they are true, every one of them."

CHAPTER EIGHTY-ONE

Tennessee Football

I am a huge fan of University of Tennessee Football. I'm of the opinion that heaven is splashed with bright orange and the first thing we'll hear when we get there is "Rocky Top"! Disagree? Then get your own vision of heaven...

Since our church offers worship on Saturday night there are times when I have to miss the big game. Such was the case one weekend when UT was playing the University of Georgia. The winner would have the inside track to the division title and excitement was running fever pitch.

What's a Big Orange fan to do? Instead of calling in sick, I did the right thing and preached, but I had the forethought to tape the game on my VCR at home. My plan was to drive home quickly and watch the game as if it were a live broadcast.

My plan was short-circuited, however, when a guy yelled to me across the church parking lot: "Hey, how 'bout them Vols? Can you believe they won?"

This turned out to be a blessing in disguise. As I watched the tape, it was obvious Tennessee didn't have their "A

Game." But it didn't upset me. Why? I already knew the final score. They missed a tackle. So what. They fumbled. Big deal. The pressure was off because I knew in the end the Vols would win.

It dawned on me I was witnessing a wonderful spiritual analogy. You see, I've read the back of the Book. In the end, guess who wins in the battle for eternity? Yep. We do!

So we throw an interception. So we fail to convert on fourth down. So we stumble throughout life. In the end... because of the cross...we win anyway!

[Cf. Revelation 19-22]

CHAPTER EIGHTY-TWO

The Tooth Fairy and Jesus

I'm a skeptic. I don't believe in the Loch Ness Monster, the Tooth Fairy or the Easter Bunny. I don't believe Elvis is alive and working at Taco Bell. I don't believe in space aliens primarily because they always seem to appear to toothless farmers in Idaho instead of scientists at MIT.

I thought of Christianity in the same terms. I thought faith was a purely emotional experience renounced by anyone with more than two brain cells to rub together. I thought a typical church service consisted of a fat preacher in a polyester suit, old ladies with beehive hairdos shouting "amen brother" and lots of snotty-nosed kids making airplanes with the offering envelopes. After whooping it up for an hour, everybody went home and ate fried chicken.

I thought faith was the hope that something was true even though you knew it probably wasn't. So I wondered, "How can these people base their life on something that can't be proven?"

Then I encountered a new definition of faith. I discovered that real faith can be tried, tested and proven.

173

For example, Hebrews 11:1 says, "Faith is the **evidence** of things unseen, the **substance** of things hoped for." These words are judicial terms, commonly used to categorize solid testimonials that could stand up under cross examination.

Don't believe me? Wonderful! Then examine the claims of Jesus for yourself. Put the Bible under a microscope. Ask all the tough questions. Dig for the answers. Guess what you'll find? You'll find what I did...God.

CHAPTER EIGHTY-THREE

What to do when Your Hut is Burning

The only survivor of a shipwreck was washed up on a small, uninhabited island. He prayed feverishly for God to rescue him. Every day he scanned the horizon, looking for help, but there was never any indication that God had heard his prayer.

As his time on the island grew, he gathered his strength and managed to build a little hut out of driftwood. This protected him from the elements and gave him a place to store his meager possessions.

One day after scavenging for food, he came home to find his little hut in flames, the smoke rolling up to the sky. Devastated, he sat in the hot sand in stunned and grief-stricken silence. With tears streaming down his face, he looked up to the heavens and screamed, "God! Why did you let this happen to me? I've served you faithfully and prayed diligently and this is how you repay me?"

Early the next day, the man was awakened by the sound of a ship approaching the island. It was a navy cruiser that had come to rescue him. "How did you know I was here?"

asked the man of his rescuers. "We saw your smoke signal" they said.

It's easy to get discouraged when things are going bad. When everything around us is crumbling and our prayers don't seem to be going any higher than the ceiling, the tendency is to give up. But don't lose heart. Just remember…the next time your "hut is burning," it just may be the smoke signal that summons the grace of God.

God is our refuge and strength, and everpresent help in times of trouble. Therefore, we will not fear…

Psalm 46:1-2

CHAPTER EIGHTY-FOUR

Oops!

"Oops" is my normal response whenever I'm careless. And normally, "oops" is a sufficient enough response to match the consequences.

Sometimes, however, "oops" is not enough. Like in "wardrobe malfunctions" (Super Bowl Half-time shows) or "dangling chads" (Al Gore vs. George W. Bush). The consequences in this case mandate a greater and more meaningful reaction.

For example, in 1989 Pierre Charmet became famous. His first claim to fame was that he was the most prolific parachutist in history. His 14,000 jumps put his name in the Guinness Book of World Records.

His second claim to fame came on Monday February 19, 1989. It was the date of Pierre's last jump. His chute didn't open—so much for the record books.

The medical examiner ruled out foul play. Pierre, you see, always packed his own chute. But this time he got careless, and nobody said "oops."

Christians are taught to pack their own chutes. Galatians 6:5 says, "Each one should bear their own load." So no matter how many times we "pack our parachutes" we must be mindful that <u>this</u> time is the most important time. We cannot afford even one moment of carelessness.

Carelessness can be a killer, a killer of one's self-respect, relationships, and testimony before the world. So pay attention my friends. The consequences are more lasting than you think. And "oops" just won't do.

CHAPTER EIGHTY-FIVE

Living in Competing Worlds

Some years ago, before the death of Mother Theresa, a television special depicted the grim human conditions that were a part of her daily life. It showed all the horror of the slums of Calcutta and her love for these destitute people. The producer interviewed her as she made her rounds in that dreadful place.

Throughout the program, commercial after commercial interrupted the flow of discussion. As I sat in my living room watching the show, I noticed the relationship (or lack of relationship) between the ads and the subject of the documentary. Here is the sequence of the topics surrounding Mother Theresa and the commercials that aired in between interviews:

A discussion of the plight of lepers (bikinis for sale); the tragedy of mass starvation (designer jeans); the state of agonizing poverty in India (Chevy trucks); the human brokenness of abandoned babies (ice cream sundaes) and the loneliness inherent in the death of the diseased (diamond watches).

The irony was so apparent. I was witnessing two different worlds in the same hour long television broadcast. There they were on display—the world of the poor and the world of the affluent.

Our culture teaches us to live as the Rich Man in the story of Lazarus. We occasionally see the poor man at the gate but we are immediately reminded of the next car or set of clothes we ought to buy.

Heaven will be the ultimate reversal of fortune. One day we will wake up to the fact that we have separated ourselves from the struggles of others and in so doing, we've missed a chance to be the healing, helping hands of God. I just hope we wake up sooner rather than later.

CHAPTER EIGHTY-SIX

The Secret to Staying Young

Someone sent me this email recently. The author is anonymous, but I love it and want to share it with you. It's titled, "How to Stay Young:"

1. Throw out all nonessential numbers. This will include age, weight, and height. Let the doctor worry about them. That's why you pay him/her.
2. Keep only cheerful friends. The grouches pull you down and they're not really your friends anyway.
3. Keep learning. Learn about the computer, crafts, gardening, whatever. Never let your brain idle. "An idle mind is the devil's workshop," and the devil's name is Alzheimer's.
4. Enjoy the simple things.
5. Laugh often, long, and loud. Laugh until you have to gasp for breath.
6. Let the tears happen. Endure, grieve, and move on. The only one with you your entire life is you. Be ALIVE while you are alive.

7. Surround yourself with what you love, whether it's family, pets, keepsakes, music, plants, or hobbies. Your home is your refuge and no one else's.

8. Cherish your health: If it is good, preserve it. If it is unstable, improve it. If it is beyond what you can improve, get help.

9. Don't take guilt trips. Take a trip to the mall, to the next county, to a foreign country, but never to where the guilt is.

10. Tell the people you love that you love them, at every opportunity.

AND ALWAYS REMEMBER: Life is not measured by the number of breaths we take but by the number of moments that take our breath away!

CHAPTER EIGHTY-SEVEN

Judging Others

Matthew 7:1-5 asks a very pointed question: Who has the right to judge? Notice I said the <u>right</u>, not <u>ability</u>. I'm certainly not volunteering to answer. I have enough trouble keeping my own life straight.

Jesus used a humorous analogy to stress the same point. He told a parable of a man with a rafter in his eye who criticized another man bothered by a speck of sawdust! In explaining this parable, Jesus said that what compounds the absurdity of this too human response is we often judge others before we have all the facts. We don't know the heart or the motives of another person, so we'd do well to concentrate on our own weaknesses before pointing out someone else's.

Steve Covey tells a not so humorous story of a man and his children who entered a New York subway car. The kids were so loud and rowdy they disturbed every passenger aboard. The father sat down and closed his eyes, seemingly oblivious to the situation. Meanwhile, his children ran back and forth, throwing things, even grabbing people's papers. It was extremely disruptive, yet the father did nothing.

Finally, another passenger turned to the man and said, "Sir, I wish you'd control your children a little better and teach them to be less unruly." The man looked up and said, "Oh, sorry. You're right. I suppose I should do something. You see, we just came from the hospital where their mother died about an hour ago. I guess I was in a daze, wondering what to do next."

I'm considering a vow of silence. I sure don't want God judging me as strictly as I judge others.

CHAPTER EIGHTY-EIGHT

The Search for Beauty and Greatness

E very summer we save our pennies and spend a week in Hilton Head Island, SC. Hilton Head is one of my favorite places in the whole wide world. It is gorgeous and the golf isn't bad either! Whenever we go to Hilton Head, we make it a point to get up early and be the first people on the beach. There's just something magnificent about seeing the sunrise over the ocean first thing in the morning, don't you think?

Another one of our favorite places is the Grove Park Inn in Asheville, NC. It's a beautiful resort hotel with fountains and rich woods and a fireplace big enough to use as a parking space. But the thing that makes it so special to me is the spectacular view of the mountains and its proximity to the Blue Ridge Parkway. One of my friends calls it "eye candy."

I believe God created within each of us a longing for eye candy. Whenever we see greatness and beauty for ourselves, whether it's an ocean or a river or a mountain range, we're awestruck by it.

This is what makes the irony of the human condition so remarkable. We can see God's creative genius all around us and still ignore the Source of that genius. Romans 1 says: "Since the creation of the world God's invisible qualities—His eternal power and divine nature—have been clearly seen" (v. 20).

Perhaps you are searching for greatness and beauty. If so, let me challenge you to open your heart as you open your eyes. For when you really, really look at the wonder of the world around you, you'll be drawn into asking life's ultimate questions: Is there a God? Why am I here? The answer to both those questions is a lot closer than you think.

CHAPTER EIGHTY-NINE

Gritting Your Teeth

When I first became a Christian I assumed those who had spiritual credentials (seminary degree, published authors, vested with a TV show) could be trusted. Even though I trusted these guys, when I heard them talk about Christianity it didn't sound like a lot of fun. In fact it sounded like a duty to keep a lot more than a joy to be experienced. I'm not saying their instruction was totally wrong, but it wasn't complete either.

Instead of seeing my life as a partnership with Jesus with his Spirit providing the power, I thought the weight of responsibility was solely on me. Instead of relying on God to work through me, I trusted my salvation to self-effort. I gritted my teeth, I lowered my shoulder and I tried to grind out my faith. There wasn't a lot of joy or hope or life to found there.

Then I was led to Romans 8:1, which says, "There is now no condemnation for those who are in Christ Jesus." I thought about that. If I am not condemned now (even though I've got a lot of work to do) I can rest in Him and rely on Him and trust in Him completely. He can make me someone I'm not and ensure that I won't be condemned in the future either. The operative phrase for me was "in Christ." I realized if I was in Christ and no longer condemned, then I'd placed myself under **self-inflicted condemnation**. I hadn't behaved badly, I had believed badly.

Listen to me. Faith isn't so much you doing something great for God. It's God doing something great in you! I didn't know that truth and as a result, I was miserable when I didn't have to be. I should have trusted in God more and in Craig a lot less.

CHAPTER NINETY

The Measure of Your Life

Ephesians 5:15 challenges us to, "be careful how we live." We know we should treat life with care, especially since it's so short. We know the measure of our life is not in what we produce but in who we live for (God and others). So, how do you measure up?

This question reminds me of the conversion of Charles Finney, a young law student. One day Charles sat in a law office in upstate New York. It was very early in the day and he was all alone when God began to deal with him. Finney said it was as if he could hear God speaking directly to him.

God: "Finney, what are you going to do when you finish your coursework?" Finney: "I'll join a firm and begin practicing law." God: "Then what?" Finney: "Get rich." God: "Then what?" Finney: "Raise a family." God: "Then what?" Finney: "Retire." God: "Then what?" Finney: "Die." God: "Then what?" The words came trembling… "Face You."

Finney was struck by the shallowness of his plans. He almost ran to the woods a half-mile away. There he stayed all day. He prayed and vowed he would not leave until he had made his peace with God. He thought about the fact that for four years he had studied law and now the vanity of a selfish life, lived only for pride and possessions, was made clear.

Finney came out of those woods with a new resolve. From that moment on he lived with the high purpose of honoring God. For the next 50 years, God used him to bring untold numbers of people to faith in Christ. He died, one of God's greatest ambassadors.

What or who are you living for? How much godly care and forethought goes into your life?

CHAPTER NINETY-ONE

Time Constraints

Time is a precious possession. We know that, we just don't live like it. We "spend" our time instead of "investing" it. Paul confronts this dilemma in Eph. 5:16: "Make the most of every opportunity."

With that Bible verse as our backdrop, see if you find yourself in these descriptions:

1. My desk (or home) is cluttered—Every surface is covered with papers, memos, or unfinished business. Cleaning up is a treasure hunt.
2. My car is dirty inside and out—Maintenance is ignored or forgotten. [Side Note: If nuclear war were declared I'd run straight to my car. There's enough food between the seats to last a lifetime.]
3. My self-esteem has hit the skids—I'm so disorganized I'm afraid that others will think I'm either lazy or mentally challenged.

4. My day doesn't belong to me—It belongs to those who cry the loudest, are the most demanding, or can manipulate me most effectively.

5. My day is spent daydreaming, instead of decision-making—I do small, boring things just so something will get done.

6. My time alone with God stinks—No one has to tell me the value of prayer, study and worship. I know those exercises are important. I just don't "exercise" like I should. I make excuses I know aren't valid.

Every minute of life holds a choice: (1) Time is a friend, a strategic, God-orchestrated opportunity to grow. (2) Time is the enemy, a constant reminder of poor planning and lack of discipline.

So, will you rise to the challenge and invest your time or continue to languish in defeat and just spend it? It's your choice.

CHAPTER NINETY-TWO

The Problem with Perfection

In Phil. 3:12, Paul says, "I'm not perfect." Now, that's noteworthy since Paul was the leading Christian of his day, a church starter, the author of 2/3 of the New Testament and an apostle. He was like Billy Graham and Mother Teresa rolled into one!

This snapshot of Paul's life reminds us that as useful as we may be in God's kingdom none of us have "arrived." We are not all we could be. The Bible says any temptation that comes our way is "common to man" (1 Cor. 10:12). That's why we need a Savior. Why? Because we need saving!

Many of us live with expectations of perfection. We set unrealistic goals for ourselves, we push and shove thinking if we can just be "holy" enough we'll earn God's approval. Even when we're depressed and burned out and suicidal, we hold onto that lie.

This obsession with perfection is not only unbiblical, it creates a no-win scenario. Even if you're able to attain some of your goals, you'll say, "That's what I should have done. It's no big deal." And if you fall short, no doubt you'll think, "What's wrong with me? What an idiot I am. Can't I do anything right?"

People who strive for perfection see God as a harsh judge who only exists to punish them. I used to think that way too. But then I discovered grace, God's unconditional love. This is how the Bible describes it: "God showed His love for us by sending Christ to die for us while we were still sinners" (Rom. 5:8). God loved us even when we didn't deserve it. And He loves you now, even though you don't deserve it. Are you perfect? Didn't think so. Do you have to be? Not really. Perfect? Nope. Forgiven? You bet!

CHAPTER NINETY-THREE

It's Spiritual to be Silly

Have you noticed the strange way perfectly normal, rational people act when they get on an elevator? It's like there's a sign in there that reads: NO TALKING. NO SMILING. NO EYE CONTACT!

Well, I'm not good at following rules as you've probably guessed by now.

Several years ago, on a trip to St. Louis, I got on an elevator, and with the conspiratorial assistance of a friend, I had a little fun. After a few fake coughs, my friend asked, for the sake of the other passengers: "The doctor gave you permission to go out in public?" I responded: "He said as long as I avoided closed spaces, I'd be fine."Guess what happened when the elevator stopped? That's right. A mass exodus baby!

Why would a professional minister with graduate degrees act so silly? Answer: Why not? I think life is filled with fun and I don't want to miss any of it, even if I have to manufacture some of it myself. So I'm silly. So what? Too many people, especially Christians, are way too serious.

To me, the abundant life includes some goofy, "what the heck" moments. I refuse to live an isolated, overly serious existence. I want to risk and feel and express whatever is joyful and life-giving and fun—for God's glory. That's right, His glory!

I think God is honored when we live life to the fullest. I think He belly laughs when His children say silly things and tell stupid jokes. The rest of society may be on the threshold of boredom with constricted emotions and sour faces, but I'm going to jump up and down like a kid and splash around in the joy of His grace. Oh, excuse me—here comes my elevator.

CHAPTER NINETY-FOUR

Better than Overtime Pay

In 1996, during Bill Clinton's re-election bid, the president's advisor, James Carville, did a masterful job focusing the attention of the electorate with this phrase: "It's the economy stupid!" Why did this work so well? Carville recognized that by and large we are led by our pocketbooks and not much else.

Now let's transfer that principle. What is our motivating force in life? If the answer is nothing more than "making a buck," then we are no different from those who don't know Jesus—and it will show. But what if our lives go deeper than that? What if our focal point is spiritual and personal? What if our motivation is integrity—for the Lord's sake?

- What if we based our work ethic on principle and not a paycheck?
- What if we said NO to a shortcut and did the job right?
- What if we determined to keep our word and lived true to our promises?

- What if we refused to profit by means that were deceptive or dishonest?

I'm reminded of a quote from Peter Drucker who said, "The best and truest evidence of success is not based on what a person does or what a person owns. It is determined by who a person is." Amen Peter!

The fact of the matter is we <u>can</u> be people of integrity. Our words <u>can</u> be seasoned with wisdom. Our work ethic <u>can</u> be above reproach. Our attitudes <u>can</u> reflect the holy calling on our lives. And the promise from God, if we embrace integrity, is that we will "receive your full inheritance" from Him. And that, my friends, is a lot more satisfying than overtime pay.

> Let your light so shine before men that they see Your good work and praise your Father in heaven.
>
> Matthew 5:16

CHAPTER NINETY-FIVE

God's Way of Doing Things

"My thoughts are not your thoughts, neither are your ways my ways," says the Lord (Isaiah 55:8).

One day, Elisabeth Elliott, a famous missionary, visited a Sunday School classroom of children. The teacher said, "Tell Ms. Elliot what God used to make the first man." One small boy shouted, "Dirt!" "That's right" said the teacher. "And what did He do next?" The boy said, "He blowed sense into him!"

I often need the sense "blowed" into me too. I'm too stubborn or too short-sighted to see that my way of doing things is not always God's way of doing things.

Take, for example, the story of the blind man in John 9. Jesus is about to heal this guy and everyone around Him knows it. Now, let's suppose you and I had been there. We'd press in to get a better look. We'd lift our children on our shoulders so they could see the miracle take place. We'd kindly ask the lady in front to remove her hat. What great thing was Jesus about to do? On tip-toed anticipation, He spit! You heard me. Jesus spit!

How's that for pomp and ceremony? That's one of the great things about Jesus. He is so unpretentious. We can become so horribly pompous in church, but Jesus never concerned himself with any of those things. In this case, He spat in the dirt. Then He made clay of the mixture and then spread it on the man's face. How's that for a miracle?

Do you want God to be busy in your life? Do you want some sense "blowed" into you? If so, don't be surprised if God uses something that may seem illogical.

CHAPTER NINETY-SIX

If You're Gonna Have a Party...

Years ago when Johnny Carson was the host of "The Tonight Show," he interviewed an eight year old boy who was a local legend in his West Virginia town. As Johnny questioned the boy, it became apparent the young man was a Christian. So Johnny asked him if he attended Sunday School. When the boy said he did Johnny inquired, "And what have you learned in Sunday school?"

"Last week our lesson was about when Jesus went to a wedding and turned water into wine" the boy said. The audience roared with laughter, but Johnny tried to keep a straight face. He said, "And what did you learn from that Bible story?" The boy squirmed in his chair as he thought about it. Then he lifted his face and said proudly, "If you're gonna have a party, be sure to invite Jesus!"

I wish more Christian felt like that little boy. I wish we would look at life through eyes of wonder and excitement instead of doom and gloom. "That's easy for you to say preacher. You don't know the pain and misery I've encountered in my life." And that's true. I don't know your pain and misery. I don't know all the turmoil you've experienced. But I know Jesus. And I know that when Jesus is invited into a life, any life, that life becomes a place of joy and peace and eternal possibilities.

The apostle John, in describing Jesus, said: "In Him was life and that life was the light of men" (John 1:4). I know this much. That eight year old was onto something and his understanding of the nature of God can serve us well. "Inviting Jesus" into any aspect of your life means the party is about to begin!

CHAPTER NINETY-SEVEN

The Unvarnished Truth

One of the traditions at Harvard Univ. is Senior Class Chapel. On the morning of graduation, seniors gather to hear words of solace and encouragement as they leave "the Yard" to take their places in the world.

The 1998 senior class heard the unvarnished truth from the Rev. Peter Gomes. In his gentle ringing tones, the inimitable Dr. Gomes took no prisoners: "You are about to be sent out of here for good, and most of you aren't ready. The president will bid you into the fellowship of educated men and women and"—here he paused each word coming slowly—"you—know—just—how—dumb—you—really—are." The senior class cheered in agreement.

"Worse than that," Gomes continued, "the world—your parents in particular—are going to expect you to be the brightest and best. But you know by noontime today, you will be out of here. By tomorrow you will be history. By Saturday, you'll be toast. That is a fact—no exceptions, no extensions."

"Nevertheless, there's reason to hope," Gomes promised. "God has not brought you this far to this place to abandon you or leave you here alone and afraid. The God of Israel never stumbles, He never sleeps and never goes on sabbatical. So, my beloved and bewildered young friends do not be afraid."

What Doctor Gomes did for that senior class at Harvard, Jesus did for the woman at the well, and a repentant David after his sin with Bathsheba, and an inconsolable Peter after having denied Christ 3 times, and—you and me after a lifetime of mistakes. Gomes had it right. "God has not brought you this far to abandon you or leave you here alone and afraid."

CHAPTER NINETY-EIGHT

A Lesson from Jimmy Carter

In his book, Living Faith, President Jimmy Carter talks about artificial, man-made barriers that divide people and give them a false sense of identity.

Having grown up in the South during the time of racial segregation, Jimmy had many African-American friends. In fact, when his parents were away he would stay with his black neighbors, Jack and Rachel Clark. He played with black friends, went fishing with them, plowed with mules side by side, and played on the same baseball team.

But when he carried water to people working the field, it was unthinkable that black workers and white workers would drink from the same dipper. As a young boy, Carter got sucked into that orientation without realizing how damaging it really was.

Looking back, President Carter is shamed by his lack of response. He should have recognized the injustice and taken a stand against it, but he didn't. Was he blind? Yes, temporarily. Although Jimmy Carter is now a champion of equal rights, he was temporarily blind to racism in the same way that many Christians are blind to the needs of those around them. Consider, for example, Matthew 25:

> I was hungry and you gave me nothing to eat, I was thirsty and you gave me nothing to drink, I was a stranger and you did not invite me in, I needed clothes and you did not clothe me, I was sick and in prison and you did not look after me. They replied, '**Lord when did we see you...?**' I tell you the truth, whatever you did not do for the least of these, you did not do for me (vv. 42-45).

CHAPTER NINETY-NINE

How Big is Your God?

Several years ago, Carl Reiner and Mel Brooks wrote a comedy sketch called "The 2013 Year Old Man". In that sketch, Reiner interviewed Brooks, who was the old gentleman. At one point, Reiner asked the old man, "Did you always believe in the Lord?"

Brooks replied: "No. We had a guy in our village named Phil and for a long time we worshiped him."

Reiner: You worshiped a guy named Phil? Why did you do that?

Brooks: Because Phil was big and mean and he could break you in two with his bare hands!

Reiner: Did you say prayers?

Brooks: Yes, would you like to hear one? It went like this. "O Phil, please don't be mean and hurt us or break us in two with your bare hands."

Reiner: So, when did you start worshiping the Lord?

Brooks: Well, one day a thunderstorm came up and a lightning bolt hit Phil. We gathered around and saw that he was dead. Then we said to each other, "Hey, there's something bigger than Phil!"

A lot of people have trouble with the obvious, namely that there's something (or someone) bigger than the creation of their own minds. And when a "lightning bolt" experience strikes, they're left looking at the dead remnant of what they used to worship.

Their god probably isn't named Phil. It may be named "career" or "dating partner" or "money," but the effect is the same. I've been there. I had to learn the hard way that my false god isn't big enough, not nearly big enough (Job 38-41).

CHAPTER HUNDRED

The Friendship Factor

reater love has no one than this…that he lay down his life for his friends" Jesus said in John 15:13. But what does it mean to "lay down your life for your friends"? The passage reveals that it involves laying aside your own concerns, your own needs, even your own reputation in deference to your friends.

You see, when Jesus spoke about friends and friendship, He spoke of relationships that had eternal consequence. And when He talked about the nature of those relationships, He wasn't talking about some vague, sentimental notion. His view toward friendship was deep and lasting, so that "laying down your life" for a friend was the norm.

Now compare Jesus' idea with how we treat so called "friends" today. When we look at modern relationships, we see just the opposite. I'm reminded of the nervous Boy Scout who stood before his troop and recited the following: "A scout obeys all to whom obedience is due and respects all duly constipated authorities."

Most of our relationships, especially those we'd place in the category of "friendship" are severely constipated. We seldom if ever function as Christ did in relationship with others and we surely don't give of ourselves in their service.

Our consumer-driven, "me-first" culture is so self-centered, we don't think of friendship as costing us anything. We've cheapened the idea of friendship and redefined it as "hanging out with people who make me feel good about myself." This is a tremendous shift away from and a blatant disregard for Jesus' challenge to "lay down your life."

Hearing God and Wearing Purple Suits

Last night I did something I rarely if ever do. I watched Christian television. True to form, an evangelist dressed in a purple suit stood on a set that looked like it was designed at Disney World and spoke about how "God spoke to him in a vision." After watching that for a few minutes I thought, "That guy is a kook." And maybe he is—but what if he's not?

If you're like me, you're cautious about such things, which I think should be applauded: "Don't believe every spirit but test them to see if they are from God because many false prophets have gone out into the world" (1 John 4:1).

Be careful. Don't believe everything you hear, but at the same time remember these words from Jesus: "**My sheep hear my voice**" (Jn 10:27). So, if you sense a holy nudge to do something or say something, don't react too quickly. Be sure to check what you think God said to you against what He's already said in the Bible. Here's why. God's will and God's word are always in perfect alignment: "The

Holy Spirit...will teach you all things and remind you of everything I have said to you" (John 14:26).

Any Christian who neglects the Bible will have great difficulty recognizing the voice of God. In addition, anyone who knows the Bible but manipulates it for selfish purposes is in danger of greater judgment.

What steps can you take to ensure you're on track? What markers can you have in place to see if others have heard from God? Here's a two-part biblical test: (1) Is the message biblical? (2) Does the message ultimately bring God glory or does it bring praise and attention to self?

The Whisper Test

Mary Ann Bird, in her book The Whisper Test, says: "I grew up knowing I was different. When I started school, my classmates made it clear to me that I looked different. I was a little girl with a misshapen lip, crooked nose, lop-sided teeth and garbled speech.

When classmates asked, "What happened to your lip?" I told tell them that I'd fallen and cut it on a piece of glass. Somehow it seemed more acceptable to have suffered an accident than to have been born that way. I was convinced that no one outside my family would love me.

There was, however, a teacher in the second grade whom we all adored—Mrs. Leonard. She was short, round, and happy.

Annually, Mrs. Leonard gave everyone a hearing test in class. Finally it was my turn. I knew from past years that as we stood against the door and covered one ear, she would sit at her desk and whisper something and we would have to repeat it. She would say things like, "The sky is blue" or "Do you have new shoes?"

When it was my turn, I waited at that door and heard words God must have put in Mrs. Leonard's mouth. I heard words that forever changed my life. Mrs. Leonard said, in her whisper, "I wish you were my little girl."

And God says to you and me and every other person deformed by sin, desperate and looking for hope: "I wish you were my child." If you stand still long enough and if you listen carefully enough, you'll hear Him whispering those words to your heart.

Work and Worship

An awful lot of Christians have "split personalities." I don't mean that in the clinical sense but in the practical sense. For example, many Christians act one way at work and another way at church. They've separated their work from their worship. But that's not how God thinks.

God sees all of life as a divine task and a holy calling. Whether you're writing a term paper, flipping burgers at McDonald's, folding laundry or sitting in an executive office downtown doesn't really matter to God and it shouldn't matter to us. God, more than a boss or Board of Directors, is the One we should look to for direction in life, including our life at work.

If you're not living a life based on this kind of **whole life worship**, you're probably caught in the trap of trying to please everybody at once. I used to be there. I felt like the guy in the circus who tried to keep all those plates spinning at the same time. Do you remember that guy? Now envision yourself at work. There's probably not much difference is there?

Mark Twain put it this way: "It's tough to climb the ladder of success, especially if you're keeping your nose to the grindstone, your shoulder to the wheel, your eye on the ball, and your ear to the ground!"

In contrast to Twain's quote, the Bible teaches that any job, no matter how mundane, can bring dignity and stability if we honor God through it. So, do you see your job as a place of worship? Is your work ethic a reflection of the character of Christ? 1 Corinthians 15:58 reminds us to "be steadfast, immovable, always abounding in the Lord knowing that your work is not in vain."

Knowing and Sharing the Truth

"Do your best to present yourself to God as one who is approved, a workman who does not need to be ashamed and who correctly handles the word of truth" (2 Tim. 2:15).

Internally, the function of the church is to know the truth; externally, the function of the church is to share the truth. In other words, the church is to make known what God prohibits and what God permits.

According to Martin Luther, the church is "the conscience of the world" and I agree. I'm not talking about setting ourselves up as super saints where we wag our fingers at everyone around us. At the same time, we must not downplay our function as "salt" and "light" in a world that is morally bland and blind.

For too long, we have sat by on our "blessed assurance" and said nothing as the world goes to "hell in a hand-basket." We've become adept at assigning people to hell and we can even describe the hand-basket that will take them there, but we haven't loved them enough to share the truth so they don't have to go in the first place!

But be warned. The uninformed will scream and say we're trying to be "morality police," but I ask you, do you really want to live in a world without a moral and ethical base? If not, where will that moral and ethical base come from? Will it come from the creation of our own minds, from the latest issue of *Cosmopolitan*, from the shifting winds of political correctness, or will it come from the Bible?

To be sure, we must be sweet and kind as we live alongside those who don't know the truth. But we must also stand for and speak forth that truth.

CHAPTER HUNDRED-FIVE

Why Does God Allow It?

Why does God allow tragedy? We've all asked that question at one time or another. Most of us know God does not CAUSE tragedy. He doesn't afflict His children (Lam. 3:33). The greater question, therefore, is why does God ALLOW these things to happen?

I'm suspicious of anyone who talks too glibly about this mystery. The fact is we will never know the answer to that question (on this side of eternity), but we can rest in the fact that God knows what is best for us; His heart is filled with love toward us, and we can trust His ways even when we don't understand them.

I recall a story my father used to share from the pulpit about some children and the death of their pet kitten. They had prayed that the cat would get well, but instead it died. They couldn't understand this, especially since they'd prayed so hard. So, they went to the local pastor. They found him in his office and asked him, "Why did God let our cat die?"

The pastor was not at all delighted to be interrupted, but out of a sense of duty, he launched into a long, complex theological response to the question. The children stood by and listened intently.

When he finished, they walked away more bewildered than before. One little boy, holding his sister's hand, looked up at her and said, "He doesn't know the answer either, does he?"

How perceptive children can be. There are so many things in this world we'll never understand. But ask yourself, "If I knew the answer, would it comfort me?" The answer, of course, is "no." What we really want is stability in the midst of tragedy and that only comes when we trust God even when we don't understand His ways.

Whiners

I don't have a lot of patience with whiners. The self-absorbed, myopic view of life drives me nuts and makes me wonder if these complainers know how blessed they really are. It reminds me of a story...

Three people arrived at the Pearly Gates. St. Peter said he had some pressing business and would they please wait? He finally came back, called one of the new arrivals in and asked if she minded waiting.

"No," she said, "I've looked forward to this for so long. I love the Lord and I can't wait to meet Jesus. I don't mind at all."

St. Peter said, "Well, I have one more question. How do you spell 'God'?" She said, "G-O-D." St. Peter said, "Go right on in."

He went outside and met another new arrival, and asked, "Did you mind waiting?"

The man said, "Oh, no. I've been a Christian for 50 years, and I'll spend eternity here. I didn't mind at all." So St. Peter said, "Just one more thing. How do you spell

'God'? "He said, "G-o-d." St. Peter said that was good and sent him into heaven.

St. Peter went back out and invited the third person in and asked her if she had minded waiting.

"As a matter of fact, I did," she replied. "I have stood in line all my life. I've waited at the supermarket, when I registered for school, when I visited the doctor's office and when I went to the movies. And I certainly resent having to wait in line for heaven!"

St. Peter said, "Well, it's perfectly normal for you to feel that way. Your complaining won't be held against you, but there is just one more question. How do you spell 'Czechoslovakia'?"

Stand Up and Be Counted!

In the movie *Scent of a Woman*, Al Pacino educates a young man on the "ways of the world." In one scene Pacino says, "There are two types of men in the world: those who stand up and are counted and those who run for cover. Cover is better."

Pacino's line has to be the motto of modern man. When the pressure is turned up, do most of us stand up for what we believe? I think you know the answer to that one and it isn't pretty is it?

I'm glad Jesus isn't like us. When given a view of the suffering that awaited Him on the cross, Jesus looked past that suffering and saw our salvation. That's why we are told to emulate His viewpoint and attitude: "who for the joy set before him endured the cross" (Hebrews 12:2).

We now know that the work of the cross and the scars resulting from it were a "joy," not for Christ, but for us, for it was His sacrificial work that brought about our spiritual renewal: "By his stripes we are healed" (Isaiah 53:6). Because of Jesus' selfless, transforming work, He had the right to say, "Whoever enters through me will be saved" (John 10:9).

Let's be honest. We've all experienced spiritual failure. We've made the wimpy choice of looking for cover instead of standing firm on our convictions.

I don't want you to be overly discouraged but isn't it true that we will almost always take the easy road? There's not a person, this author included, who can testify otherwise. We are by nature, spiritual sissies. That's why we need to be more like Jesus, a man who didn't shrink, step back, or grow silent when the heat was on!

The Key Issue: Biblical Authority

The key issue in the Christian Church today is authority: (1) what is the source of genuine authority? (2) What is our response to genuine authority? I believe this is the key issue because every day the average Christian faces a crisis of faith, a time of decision-making where he stops and asks himself, "Is there a standard, a measuring stick that can guide me in life?"

Some Christians look to their denominational heritage or the rule of a diocese. Others rely on the authority of educational achievement: "Who am I to disagree with a PhD?" they say. Still others lean on traditions and "We've always done it that way before."

I see the <u>qualified legitimacy</u> of these systems but I believe the ultimate authority for every person and every life and every situation is the Bible.

- If a diocese makes a biblically sound decision, great!
- If a learned man declares biblical integrity, great!

- If traditions are drawn from biblical truth, great!

If, however, we leave our biblical moorings, we will head down a slippery slope that leads to disaster.

This, therefore, is <u>the</u> critical issue: Is the Bible the foundation of our relationships; is it the basis of our hopes; is it the motivator of our worship or isn't it?

Psalm 1 tells us true satisfaction is only found when we take delight in an ongoing relationship with God. And how can we know about this kind relationship apart from the Bible?

Let me say that again—the goal of life is to enjoy God—and enjoying God is only possible if we know who He is and how to relate to Him (via the Bible). This is what brings fulfillment. Nothing else even comes close.

The Witness of a Wheelchair

I've known many winsome Christians who have influenced me for good and God's glory. Some of these people have suffered from physical handicaps or are prone to sickness. In spite of that, they recognize physical suffering as an opportunity to grow more powerful in the spiritual realm.

One of those friends was Mike Dunkin. Mike came to my church with a checkered background. He was a recovering alcoholic, a disabled veteran, and a spiritual skeptic. Mike had tried every form of religion you could think of, even dabbling in Wicca, an earthbased, mystical cult that worships nature.

In the midst of his search for meaning, Mike visited our church. I went to visit him in his home and instantly liked what I saw. Even though Mike was bound to a wheelchair, his mind was sharp and his wit was even sharper! After a few minutes, Mike said, "Craig, I like your church but I really don't have much use for organized religion." "Then you'll love our church," I replied, "because we're about as unorganized as you can get!" After a few more quips like that Mike and I became good friends.

Eventually, Mike became a believer in Christ. He grew in his faith through small group Bible studies, worship experiences, and personal interaction with others who were "real" in their faith.

My fondest memories involve conversations I had with Mike after worship. He always had a playful jab for me: "You didn't mess it up too bad today preacher" or "If you'd quit horsing around and pray for me, I might get out of this wheelchair."

Mike never did get out of that wheelchair, but his spirit learned to soar!

In the fall of 2002 Mike faced a complicated and risky surgery that would rid his body of cancer. As I sat beside his bed the day before his surgery Mike told me, "Craig, my trust in the Lord has never been stronger. I can't begin to tell you how thankful I am to know that I'm in good hands."

Mike never recovered from that surgery. At his memorial service tears were shed and great times of laughter were shared because it was obvious to all that this crippled veteran and one time skeptic had become a spiritual giant!

Whenever I think of Mike or the many others like him, I think of these words from the apostle Paul:

> Therefore we do not lose heart. Though outwardly we are wasting away, yet inwardly we are being renewed day by day.
>
> 2 Corinthians 4:16

Could You Make a Rabbit?

Psalm 19:8 says, "The precepts of the Lord are right, giving joy to the heart." The word right means "objectively straight, opposed to crooked." Our world is filled with crookedness: crooked hearts, minds and people. Is it any wonder, therefore, that there is so little joy in the world? Man, left to his own devices, will find or invent crookedness every time.

I was reminded of this when I read about Frank Sheed, a Catholic author, who was interrupted by a heckler during a lecture at the "Speakers Corner" in 1944. Sheed had just described the order and design of the universe, when the heckler, pointing to all the world's ills, said, "I could make a better universe than your God." Sheed paused and then replied, "I won't ask you to make a better universe, but would you make a rabbit—just to establish confidence?"

We are so stubborn, so self-absorbed, and so crooked in our hearts, that the idea of the Bible as an objective standard for life causes us to bristle. To submit to anyone (even God) or anything (even His Word) offends our platform of self-sufficiency and pride. So we grab onto the throne of our own ideas with a death grip, all the while letting go of the very thing that could straighten out our relationships, dreams and lives.

During World War II, a South Sea Islander with Bible in hand, approached a soldier to show him what he had learned about God. The GI was a skeptic and because of his lack of faith said, "I outgrew that sort of thing a long time ago." The islander responded, "It's a good thing I haven't. If it weren't for this book called the Bible, you'd be dinner tonight!"

Are You Listening?

Suppose Jesus met you on the street one day and said, "Hello, My name is Jesus, I'm the Son of God and I came to save you from your sin and give you joy and everlasting life. By My death and resurrection I've paid for all your sins. By My Spirit and through My word (the Bible) I'll help you make choices that will guarantee life's greatest blessings. Will you trust Me and follow Me?"

Suppose you said, "Well, I want to be happy. And I like the idea of having all my sins forgiven. But I've looked at some of Your directions for life and I just don't agree with some of Your ideas. So here's the deal. I think I'll accept Your forgiveness, and I really appreciate it. But I think I'll go with my own ideas on how to live."

What would Jesus say to you? Well, we know exactly what He'd say. That exact scene took place in the Bible.

A rich young man came to Jesus one day and asked Him about eternity. When Jesus gave the young man practical advice about money and life the Bible says, "he went away sad" (Matt. 19:22). It was not financial advice that made the man walk away sad; it was his unwillingness to obey what God in the Flesh had just said.

So let me ask you. Do you really expect to hear from God? If so, will you follow what He says? This is where God's grace and our obedience meet. This is where worship of God gains clarity. Yes, God forgives our inattention. Yes, God forgives all the times we've ignored His plan. But if we want to hear from Him, we have to start putting into practice what He says!

Resolutions

New Year's resolutions don't work—at least they don't work for me. It seems no sooner than I make one, I break it and then I feel like a failure. No matter how much willpower I work up I never seem to actually accomplish anything.

I wonder if all those Bible heroes we study about ever felt the way I do. Abram (we now know him as Abraham) for example, must have been confused at the very least when God spoke to him and called him to a resolution far beyond his abilities: "The Lord said to Abram, 'Leave your country, your people and your father's household and go to the land I will show you'" (Genesis 12:1).

Several factors make this call remarkable. For starters, Abram was from a culture that worshipped false gods. Second, Abram was asked to leave everything and everyone he knew (country, people and his father's household). Third, Abram didn't even know where he was going.

What did Abram do? Thankfully, for us, he obeyed God and that began a series of events that led to blessing for "all peoples on earth" (v. 3). And now to the big question, "Why did he obey?" I think one reason he obeyed was the simple fact that God was the one who offered the invitation!

Come to think of it, maybe my resolutions don't work because they are my resolutions and not God's. Maybe if I spent more time listening to God's voice instead of my own, I'd experience a lot more blessing and a lot less disappointment. I wonder if you could say the same thing.

CHAPTER HUNDRED-THIRTEEN

The Stockpile

In 2 Kings 6-7, the city of Samaria was held captive by the armies of Aram. Because of the siege, the city experienced a famine so severe it drove the people to cannibalism.

Doomed to die with the rest, four outcast lepers decided on a desperate plan—to enter the camp of the enemy and surrender: "If they spare us, we will live; if they kill us, we were going to die anyway" (7:4).

To their amazement, the lepers found the camp deserted. How did this happen? God caused the army of Aram "to hear the sound of chariots and horses and a great army" (7:6). The Arameans assumed the King of Israel had hired the Hittites and Egyptians to attack them. Terrified, they fled for their lives, leaving everything (I mean everything) behind.

The lepers were beside themselves! They rushed from tent to tent, eating everything in sight, filling their arms with silver and gold, gathering mounds of clothes. But then they stopped and thought about the folks back home: "We're

235

not doing right. We're keeping all this to ourselves. We can share this with those who are starving!"

Why did the lepers share their secret? They shared because of the "stockpile factor"—The Lord had given them too much. They couldn't use all those riches. To not share would have been a crime.

This is our mandate as Christians: to share from the stockpile of God's grace, to focus on and pray for others to be changed just like we were, to think beyond ourselves and to see an entire world in need of the love and grace of Christ.

Forgetting God's Benefits

David said, "Forget not all God's benefits" (Psa. 103:2) which must mean forgetting the benefits God is a real possibility.

When I was a kid growing up in church, the Song Director (we couldn't afford a Minister of Music) would have "Name Your Favorite Hymn" Night. Each time he did that, Sister Sue would shout, "Count Your Blessings"! I remember well singing the lyrics of that old hymn:

> When upon life's billows you are tempest tossed, when you are discouraged, thinking all is lost count your many blessings, name them one by one And it will surprise you what the Lord has done.

How could the blessings of God surprise us? The same way it's possible to forget His benefits. So let me remind you of a few of them:

- If you woke up this morning with relatively good health, you are more blessed than 6 million people who won't survive the week.
- If you attend church without fear of harassment, arrest torture or death, you have more freedom than 3 billion people in the world.
- If you have food in the refrigerator, clothes on your back, a roof over your head and a place to sleep, you are better off than 75% of the world.
- If you have money in the bank or in your wallet, you are among the wealthiest 8% of the world.

Who is the Source of all these blessings? The same Source of all of life's blessings: God! So don't be surprised by what He's done. And please don't forget that He is the One who did it!

Removing Our Sins

Psalm 103:12 says, "as far as the east is from the west, so far has he removed our sins from us."

This verse has tremendous spiritual import because to remove something "as far as the east is from the west" is a limitless standard of measure. Let me explain.

You can travel north from a given point and eventually you'll reach the North Pole, a definite point; then you can travel south to the South Pole, another definite point. East and west, on the other hand, is a different matter. You can start traveling east and there is no point at which you will start to travel west. No matter how long you continue, there is no point at which you will start to travel west.

What Psalm 103:12 tells us is that God takes our sins (no matter how heinous) and removes them from us infinitely and we will never, ever see the full, eternal weight of them!

In the classic poem, "The Rime of the Ancient Mariner," Coleridge depicts an albatross which accompanies a ship and brings favorable winds—a good omen. But one of the sailors shoots the bird, and the winds die along with the bird. As punishment, the dead bird is hung around the neck of the sailor as a reminder of his foolishness.

The lingering question is, "What albatross do you have around your neck? When the scars of sin are your constant companion, what remedy do you have?" If you aren't in relationship with Christ, the sad reality is you have no remedy. But if you know Him and love Him, you know the Forgiver of Sins and the Redeemer of Life and He has removed your sins from you as far as the east is from the west.

Personalized Worship

If your idea of worship is nothing more than a series of acts or words shared on the weekend, you haven't begun to worship. The biblical idea of worship is tied to a personal response to a personal God who loves and cares for those who worship Him. Anything less than that kind of response, even if we call it "worship" will be <u>duty</u> and <u>drudgery</u> instead of delight.

We all know this by experience. For example, one man retires from the firm loved and respected by his colleagues. When his retirement party is given everyone knows the hand shakes and speeches and congratulations and gold watch are sincere. They come from the heart.

Contrast that with the retirement party for a shiftless grumbler. He gets a party too. There are handshakes and speeches and a gold watch just like there was for the first guy, but everyone (including Mr. Shiftless) knows the "honor" was paid out of duty.

Listen to me. The drawing near of our heart to God equals the coming alive of our feelings for God. The psalms, for example, are filled with spontaneous expressions of raw emotions and honest feelings.

This makes me wonder why there is an odd suspicion of emotions in mainline churches. There are those who falsely believe that emotions are not only unnecessary but a hindrance to genuine worship.

The "Frozen Chosen" can champion the idea that worship has to do with decorum in God's presence, but I reject that idea and so does God. "Taste and see that the Lord is good!" it says in Psalm 34:8. And I don't think anyone can taste the Lord without getting excited about His goodness!

To order additional copies of

Say What?

Have your credit card ready and call:

1-877-421-READ (7323)

or please visit our web site at
www.pleasantword.com

Also available at:
www.amazon.com
and
www.barnesandnoble.com

9 781414 104850

Printed in the United States
70648LV00002B/37